Welcome to the Flower Fairy Garden!

Where are the fairies?
Where can we find them?
We've seen the fairy-rings
They leave behind them!

Is it a secret
No one is telling?
Why, in your garden
Surely they're dwelling!

No need for journeying,
Seeking afar:
Where there are flowers,
There fairies are!

FREDERICK WARNE

Published by the Penguin Group
Penguin Books Ltd, 80 Strand, London WC2R 0RL, England
Penguin Young Readers Group, 345 Hudson Street,
New York, New York 10014, U.S.A.
Penguin Books Australia Ltd, 250 Camberwell Road, Camberwell,
Victoria 3124, Australia
Canada, India, New Zealand, South Africa

1 3 5 7 9 10 8 6 4 2

First published by Frederick Warne & Co., 2006-2007
This edition first published 2009
This edition copyright © Frederick Warne & Co., 2009

New reproductions of Cicely Mary Barker's illustrations
copyright © The Estate of Cicely Mary Barker, 1990
Original text and illustrations copyright
© The Estate of Cicely Mary Barker,
1923, 1925, 1926, 1934, 1940, 1944, 1948

ISBN-13: 978 0 72326 389 0

Printed in China

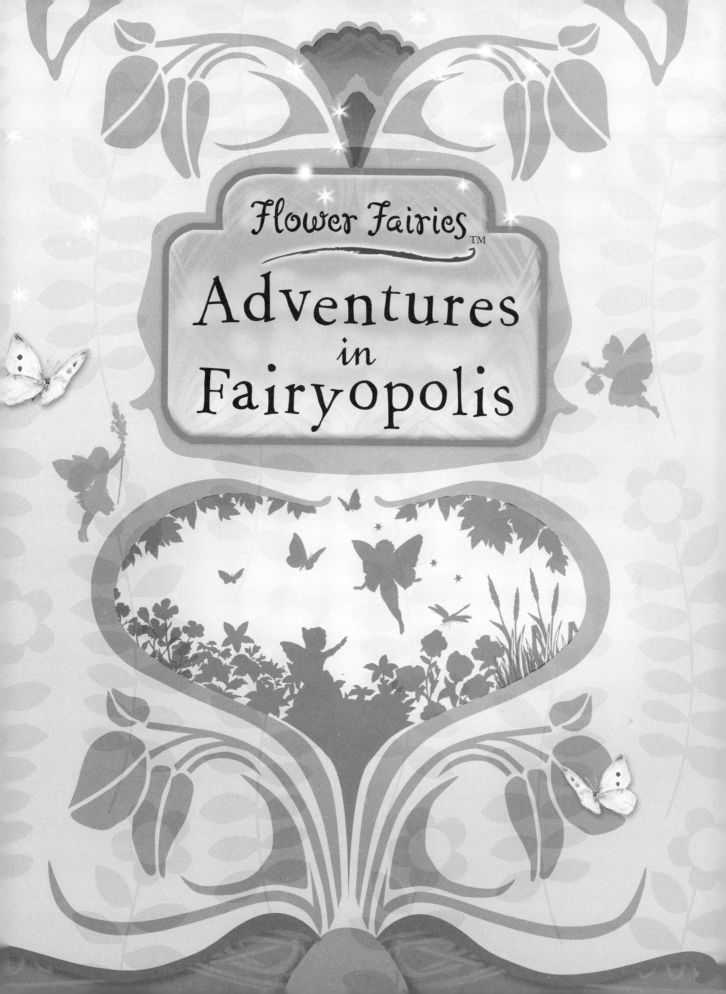

Flower Fairies™
Adventures
in
Fairyopolis

Contents

Lavender's Midsummer Mix-up

Rose's Special Secret

Strawberry's New Friend

Candytuft's Enchanting Treats

Buttercup and the Fairy Gold

The Song of
the Lavender Fairy

"Lavender's blue, diddle diddle"—
    So goes the song;
All round her bush, diddle diddle,
    Butterflies throng;
(They love her well, diddle diddle,
    So do the bees;)
While she herself, diddle diddle,
    Sways in the breeze!
"Lavender's blue, diddle diddle,
    Lavender's green";
She'll scent the clothes, diddle diddle,
    Put away clean—
Clean from the wash, diddle diddle,
    Hanky and sheet;
Lavender's spikes, diddle diddle,
    Make them all sweet!
(The word "blue" was often used in old days
where we should say "purple" or "mauve".)

Lavender's Midsummer Mix-up

by Kay Woodward

Chapter One
Party Petals

"Phew!" Lavender heaved a huge sigh of relief and flopped down on a mossy hillock. She'd had the busiest—and best— week ever, getting ready for tomorrow's Midsummer Party, and everything was nearly done.

Lavender had the strangest of hobbies. While some Flower Fairies liked to help by stirring nutshells of fairy nectar or stringing garlands of honeysuckle and forget-me-not from branch to branch and twig to twig, she was at her happiest when up to her elbows in sparkling soapsuds.

On Monday, Lavender had scurried about the Flower Fairy Garden, reminding everyone about the Midsummer Party. Then she went back to her own beautiful flower and waited below its fragrant petals.

Soon, there was a long queue of Flower Fairies lining up to see her, each clutching a dirty, crumpled outfit and wearing an anxious smile.

"Is there anything at all you can do?" asked Elder tentatively, handing over a bundle of frothy lace that looked as if it had been dipped in mud.

"Hmm . . ." Lavender peered closely at the delicate frock. "It'll take a hefty sprinkling of fairy magic . . ." She glanced up at worried-looking Elder and smiled. "But it'll be as good as new."

"Oh, thank you," breathed the little fairy, who was just as beautiful as her dress.

Next came Sycamore, who was well known for his treetop gymnastics. Lavender wasn't surprised to see that his leafy jacket and amber shorts were ripped to shreds. Again. Sycamore winked cheekily at Lavender, who tutted and dropped his rags on top of Elder's dress.

"Next!" she said briskly, wondering where she had put her thistle needle and dandelion thread.

By Tuesday, the teetering pile of party laundry had become taller than Lavender, and she couldn't help feeling slightly nervous about the huge task that loomed ahead. Shaking long, dark curls from her face, she collected tablets of her own special lavender soap.

Suddenly, the air filled with a snowy fluttering of wings, and Lavender looked up, first with surprise and then with delight, to see her best friends.

"You're here!" she exclaimed as the swarm of white butterflies enveloped her in a ticklish hug. Without even waiting to be asked, they zoomed toward the dirty clothes, and in seconds a very strange procession was winding its way toward the stream—first Lavender, then a bobbing row of petal bonnets, dainty shoes, and other assorted items of fairy clothing, each carried by a dazzling white butterfly.

"Thank you!" cried Lavender, as the butterflies waved good bye. She dunked the first garment into the clear water, catching a glimpse of yellow out of the corner of her eye. She knew that this was Iris, a sweet but shy fairy who lived at the water's edge.

Lavender didn't call out, knowing that Iris would venture over when she was ready.

* * *

By Wednesday, all the Flower Fairy party clothes had been rubbed and scrubbed and scrubbed and rubbed clean. And Lavender and Iris were firm friends.

"So you really, truly do *enjoy* doing this?" asked Iris, who was having great difficulty understanding the idea that Lavender did laundry for fun. Iris was a very pretty fairy. The sunlight made her glossy auburn hair look extra-shiny, while her glorious yellow dress simply shone.

Lavender shrugged dispiritedly. "I have no choice, really," she said. "Not until the elves lift the wicked charm that binds me to a life of soap and—" Unable to keep a straight face for a second longer, she giggled loudly at Iris's horrified expression. "I don't suppose you're any good at hanging out clothes . . . ?" she added quickly.

"Of course!" replied Iris, jumping down to the riverbank to lend a hand.

Politely, Lavender asked the spiders if they could provide the washing lines. They were happy to oblige and were soon reeling out lengths of glistening gossamer, which Lavender stretched from flower to flower. Soon, sparkling clean party petals were flapping gently on the lines.

* * *

On Thursday, instead of taking a day off while the warm breeze dried the beautiful outfits, Lavender had been busier than ever.

She realized that her stocks of lavender-scented soap were running low and that they'd be much in demand before the Midsummer Party—the one event when everyone wanted to smell extra-specially delicious.

She gathered together her ingredients: three hundred and sixty-five lavender petals, to make soap that would smell fragrant on every day of the year; a sprinkling of fairy dust, to make sure the soap made whatever it touched magically clean; and a buttercup filled to the brim with dew, to bind everything together.

Lavender dropped all of the ingredients into a beechnut shell and, using a long stem from her own flower, stirred vigorously until everything had dissolved. Then, she poured the mixture into tiny nutshell molds and left them to set. Nothing was wasted—even the leftover drops were used to make a beautiful scent for the lucky Flower Fairies to dab on their wrists.

13

* * *

On Friday morning, the rising sun had revealed a kaleidoscope of dazzling color. Row upon row of fine garments, made from the prettiest petals, leaves, berries, and seeds that the Flower Fairy Garden had to offer, billowed in the breeze.

"Do you know what?" said Iris thoughtfully, "If you squint a bit, you can't see the purply-red stain on Elderberry's frock at all."

Lavender was shocked. How could she have let this happen? She'd been so careful! She tore across the grass, skidding to a halt before Elderberry's spotless dress . . . and heard Iris giggling gleefully behind her.

"Only teasing!" called Iris, delighted to have caught Lavender out.

That'll teach me, thought Lavender with a chuckle.

And now that everything really was clean, there was one finishing touch for Lavender to make. She picked a stem from her own flower—one with a plump cluster of flowers at its tip—and shook it near the billowing outfits, releasing tiny spikes of lavender laden with her own special fragrance.

* * *

Somehow, Lavender had drifted off to sleep. She creaked open her tired eyelids and sat upright on the mossy hillock. It was still Friday. She looked to make sure that the party outfits were still there. They were.

She glanced at the dandelion clock nearby. Its huge downy head was still half-full of floaty seeds, which meant that there was plenty of time before she had to gather and fold the clothes for tomorrow's party.

Like a jack-in-the-box, Lavender sprang to her feet. Then, she cupped her hands around her mouth and bellowed loudly, in a most unfairylike way. "Lavender's blue, diddle diddle!"

They were strange words indeed for a Flower Fairy who'd always considered her flower to be lilac, mauve, or—when the sun had set—deepest purple, but according to ancient fairy tradition, this color had always been known as "blue".

And it didn't really matter to Lavender, because she knew that whatever color anyone thought it was, her flower would always smell as sweet.

In a flash, a cloud of bees swarmed toward Lavender. Distracted for a moment by the party clothes, they wove in and out of the gossamer washing lines, nuzzling the fragrant petals. "Bzzzzzz . . ."

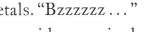

they said approvingly.

Hot on their heels were the butterflies, who alighted playfully on Lavender's shoulders, whispering secrets of the world beyond the Flower Fairy Garden to her.

A dandelion seed floated past Lavender's nose, reminding her that time was passing and spurring her into action. "Let's play a game!" she said to her hovering, dancing audience.

"Hide-and-seek?"

The bees hummed happily, while the butterflies flapped their wings in agreement.

"So who'll be . . . ?" Lavender realized that she was speaking to thin air—"it," she finished. "Looks like it'll be me, then." But, like all the other Flower Fairies in the garden, she was an obliging creature, who so loved to take part in any game that she didn't mind which part she played. She ran lightly toward the nearest flower bed, fluttering into the air with excitement every few steps.

Spotting that the snapdragons were trembling suspiciously, she crept closer and peered inside. Sure enough, the bees had dived into the cushiony yellow blossoms, where they were busy sampling the delicious nectar.

"You're it!" sang Lavender.

There was a single lazy buzz by way of reply, and it dawned on her that hide-and-seek might not be the best game to play with a swarm of thirsty bees . . .

When it was Lavender's turn to hide, she knew just the place—among the petals of her very own flower! With her lovely lilac dress she would blend right in, and surely no one would dream that she'd hide here. It was just too obvious!

So she shook her wings, took a deep breath, and—with a sparkling burst of Flower Fairy magic—flew right to the tallest stems of lavender. And she might be hiding there still, if a troublesome leaf hadn't tickled her nose.

'Aaa . . . Aaa . . . Achoo!' she sneezed, and was discovered immediately by a passing butterfly.

The butterflies had thought of an extra-clever hiding place. They darted past the white narcissus, ignoring wild bindweed in the nearby hedge, and pretended to be pretty white dresses dancing on the washing line!

"Be careful!" warned Lavender, who had been keeping a nervous eye on her precious laundry. But the butterflies told her not to worry. They knew just how long it had taken her to make everything clean, and they weren't going to spoil it.

While Lavender had been chasing in and out of the plants and flowers, word had spread throughout the Flower Fairy Garden. Now a small crowd of curious onlookers had gathered to watch the merriment.

"Hello, Lavender!" called Periwinkle, a flaxen-haired fairy dressed in a dusky blue tunic and sage green leggings. "Room for one more?"

"Of course!" puffed Lavender, leaning against a sturdy geranium stalk to catch her breath.

"May I?" added Fuchsia. At Lavender's nod, she performed a neat pirouette, sending her pink and purple petticoats spinning outwards.

"And me?" Zinnia—who was always brimming with energy—flapped her beautiful butterfly wings and fluttered to join them.

It had to be the best morning ever. They played tag and leapfrog. They raced one another. Then Lavender had a brainstorm— the Flower Fairy Garden was a ready-made obstacle course! So they chased one another around bushes, and leaped over streams. It was just what everyone needed after a week of party preparations.

"Look at me!" cried Periwinkle as he looped-the-loop around a climbing plant laden with pink and lilac flowers.

"Shhhhh!" hushed Sweet Pea from a leafy perch. She raised a finger to her lips and pointed to a cluster of flowers where baby Flower Fairy Sweet Peas were snoozing. "You'll wake the little ones!"

"Ooops!" whispered Periwinkle. "Sorry about that!" He rocketed back down to the garden, landing with a thud.

Lavender winced. "Be careful," she said. "You won't be able to dance at the Midsummer Party with a sprained ankle." She turned back to the obstacle course, spying Zinnia and Fuchsia weaving in and out of the tulips.

The ground shook.

"Periwinkle," Lavender said automatically, "whatever you're doing, be sure to take care."

"Huh?" said Periwinkle.

Lavender turned to see him sitting cross-legged on the bare earth, snacking on a ripe hazelnut. The ground shook again, louder now. Whoever or whatever was making the thudding noise, it wasn't Periwinkle. So, gathering all her courage, Lavender bravely peeped around a prickly hawthorne bush and caught her breath at what she saw . . .

Strolling over the lawn toward them were two human children, so tall that they blocked out the sun. The loud noise was the sound of a huge black-and-white ball that they were bouncing as they walked.

Thud! Thud-thud!

Lavender shrank back into the shadows of the hawthorne bush, accidentally pricking herself on a spike and then muffling the squeak of pain in case they heard her.

"Sam, what's that?" said a girl with auburn hair, a dusting of freckles, and a heart-shaped face. "I'm sure I saw something twinkle. Do you think it could be a fairy . . . ?"

Her heart sinking, Lavender patted the folds of her petal dress, realizing instantly that her precious handful of fairy dust that she kept for emergencies was gone. The girl must have spotted it shining in the grass.

"Let's go and investigate!" said the other child, a boy with ruffled blond hair. "Hurry up, Milly!"

And, curious eyes fixed firmly on the ground, they crept straight toward the bottom of the garden—and the Flower Fairies.

Chapter Three
Visitors

Lavender thought back quickly over the Flower Fairy Law that every fairy was taught as soon as they were old enough … Humans—especially children—were known to be very inquisitive creatures, who had long suspected that fairies lived in their world. But if humans knew that fairies really did exist, right under their noses, the Flower Fairies' world would be in danger of discovery. Which was why they must stay out of sight at all times.

It was time for a real-life game of hide-and-seek. Keeping under cover of the shadowy bushes, Lavender tiptoed over to where the other Flower Fairies were huddled beneath a large, leafy plant.

"Wait until you hear my splendid plan," said Periwinkle, who wasn't scared of anything. "Hiding under this—" he snapped off a dark green leaf— "I can smuggle all the Flower Fairies to safety, one by one." He looked proudly around the group as if expecting a round of applause.

"That really is a splendid plan," said Lavender, careful not to hurt his feelings, "but it's a little risky. The human children will be suspicious of anything and everything that moves."

"Ah, yes," said Periwinkle, nodding sensibly. "So what do you suggest?"

"We must hide," said Lavender. Quickly, she told her fairy friends to find a hiding place and stay there—no matter how close the humans came. Most importantly, they must stay absolutely still.

So the Flower Fairies stole away. No one dared to fly, in case their gossamer wings were spotted shining in the afternoon sunlight.

* * *

"Do you think we're close?" whispered Milly, so loudly that the Flower Fairies—who have incredible hearing—could hear her right at the bottom of the garden.

Despite her fear, Lavender chuckled to herself. If only humans realized just how much noise they made, they might guess why fairies were so hard to find.

"The fairies are listening to us now . . . " said Sam in a spooky voice. "They're hiding under this very bush." Without warning, he reached down toward the hawthorne branches where Lavender had hidden, and swept them aside. "Boo!" he said. Then, "Ouch!", as he found out how prickly it was.

Lavender sped away. While she'd been listening to the children, a plan had begun to form in her mind—an ingenious plan that would keep Flower Fairy Garden safe and keep the human children happy. But first, she had to talk to the bees and butterflies. She glanced over her shoulder as huge, shiny shoes stomped into view. Faster—she must go faster!

The bees had supped the nectar from the snapdragon flowers and were now buzzing lazily nearby, full after their sticky feast.

"Hi, Snapdragon!" Lavender waved to the fairy snuggled comfortably between the blossoms. "Stay out of sight—there are humans around!" Snapdragon nodded and nestled farther into the flowery depths.

Lavender scampered quickly toward the bees, wishing for the thousandth time that she hadn't lost her fairy dust. And it took such a long time to make too . . .

Each Flower Fairy gathers pollen from their own flower, then grinds it between two rough stones until all that remains is a heap of tiny glittering particles—fairy dust. The precious dust can be used for all sorts of magical things—for summoning friendly insects and for distracting humans with its alluring sparkle. It can even be used to decorate flowers at Christmas time.

Luckily, the bees had seen Lavender, and they buzzed toward her when she called. The white butterflies came too—they had been visiting Lavender's own flowers nearby, fluttering merrily around the fragrant petals. Quickly, the Flower Fairy whispered her idea, before hurrying across to speak to Honeysuckle.

* * *

"We're never going to find anything," sighed Milly, looking wistfully at a mass of elegant roses—unwittingly overlooking the tiny fairy huddled beneath one of the flowers, her soft pink dress and wings exactly the same color as the rose itself.

Lavender too had concealed herself among her own flowers. And as she peered around the garden, her keen fairy eyes—so much sharper than human eyes —saw that the other Flower Fairies had done the same thing, their outfits providing the perfect camouflage to fool curious children.

Milly and Sam thudded closer and closer, until they were so near that she could almost touch them. A twig snapped beneath Sam's foot, as if signalling to Lavender that this was the moment to set her plan in motion. She nodded at Honeysuckle, who was balanced high on his wild, raggedy flower, swaying slightly in the breeze. He blew his flowery horn loudly.

Toot!

Milly frowned, almost as if she'd heard Honeysuckle's tiny signal, but a buzzing crowd of bees distracted her at once. They swarmed noisily into the air, where a host of white butterflies joined the throng, flitting and fluttering around crazily, like handkerchiefs waving in the distance.

Then, at another toot from Honeysuckle's trumpet … they were off! The bees and butterflies leaped from flower to flower, pausing for a moment by the trickling stream, before continuing their merry Midsummer dance around the garden.

Eagerly, the children followed, not realizing that they were being led farther and farther away from the Flower Fairies' secret world.

"Fairies at the bottom of the garden?" gasped Sam as he dashed

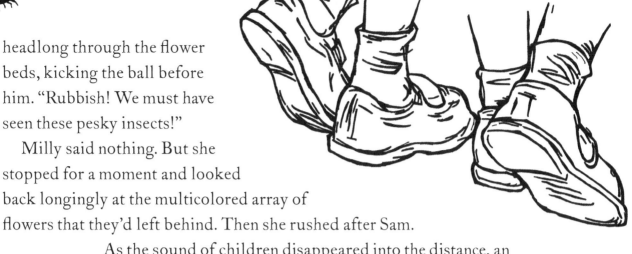

headlong through the flower beds, kicking the ball before him. "Rubbish! We must have seen these pesky insects!"

Milly said nothing. But she stopped for a moment and looked back longingly at the multicolored array of flowers that they'd left behind. Then she rushed after Sam.

As the sound of children disappeared into the distance, an amazing transformation began to take place. The charming—if slightly overgrown—garden rustled and shook into life. Here, a dainty head peeped out of a crinkly yellow blossom. There, a tiny arm stretched from behind a stem where its owner had been hiding.

Leaves were pushed aside, petals unfolded, and long grasses moved to reveal a garden full of smiling Flower Fairies.

Lavender gazed around, thrilled that her plan had worked. But her relief turned swiftly to despair as her eyes met a dreadful sight.

She gulped, closed her eyes, and then looked again.

Oh no!

Chapter Four
Disaster!

Where the gently billowing rows of bright, clean party petals had once been, there was now only a tangled mess of gossamer and flowers.

As the children had rushed headlong after the bees and butterflies, they had snapped the delicate gossamer washing lines and trampled over the Flower Fairies' party outfits. Now all of the beautiful clothes lay on the ground, covered with mud, moss, and grass stains. Worse still, some were horribly torn.

For a moment, Lavender felt frozen to the spot. Then she sank to her knees, put her face into her hands, and sobbed.

Everything is my fault, she thought. *If only I hadn't played games earlier, I wouldn't have attracted the attention of the children . . . and then I wouldn't have had to dream up my stupid plan . . . and then the bees and the butterflies wouldn't have zoomed over the washing lines . . . and then the children wouldn't have stomped over the clothes.*

Great fat tears slipped down her cheeks as she realized that all of her hard work was ruined. And with no party outfits to wear, the Midsummer Party would be ruined too. If only she'd snoozed instead. If only . . .

Lavender listened to the cries of disappointment echoing all around. She hardly dared to look—everyone was certain to be upset and so disappointed with her. But cautiously, she lifted her head.

She needn't have worried. Everyone knew that Lavender wasn't to blame for the messy clothes. And they were such kindly creatures that they didn't blame the children either. After all, how were Milly and Sam to know that they'd been racing through a miniature laundry, when the Flower Fairies kept their world so secret?

"Don't worry," said Elder, handing Lavender a handkerchief made from her own lacy blossom.

"But everything's so d-d-dirty!" wept Lavender.

"Oh, that's not such a bad thing," said a small, exceedingly grubby little fairy, only recognizable because of the sycamore seeds he was attempting to juggle with. "If you're wearing dirty clothes, you can get up to heaps more fun!"

Sycamore's giggles were infectious, and soon everybody was laughing—even Lavender. The Flower Fairies flocked around to comfort her, brimming with brilliant ideas and plans of action.

Periwinkle leapt on to a mushroom and cleared his throat importantly. "There's a whole day before the Midsummer Party," he announced. "That's plenty of time to get everything sorted. And we'll all lend a hand."

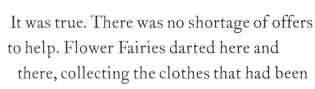

It was true. There was no shortage of offers to help. Flower Fairies darted here and there, collecting the clothes that had been scattered far and wide by the children's hasty feet.

Carefully, Lavender examined every garment before sorting them into different piles: terribly filthy, quite dirty, slightly grubby, crumpled but clean, and absolutely spotless. Lavender herself took charge of the "terribly filthy" pile, while advising other Flower Fairies on just the right amount of soap to use when cleaning their share of the party clothes.

There was one other sorry heap of petals —clothes that had been ripped so badly that a dunk in the stream would not fix them. And here, Tansy came to the rescue. With her tiny sewing kit—and a good helping of fairy dust—she mended rips and holes, neatened jagged edges, and replaced buttons and beads. Zinnia brought fresh petals for Tansy to patch the most ragged outfits.

Suddenly, there was an agonized shout from the stream, and all the Flower Fairies flung down whatever they were doing and ran to see what was amiss. The distressed sound was coming from Iris, who had been allocated a pile of slightly grubby clothes to scrub and rinse.

"What's happened now?" wailed Lavender. Had the children returned? Had Iris fallen into the river? Could today get any worse?

"I've run out of soap!" cried Iris, looking so sad that Elder began searching in her pockets for another hankie.

28

Lavender was so relieved that nothing worse was wrong, it took a moment for her to realize that this was quite a problem. Soap wasn't something that she could conjure up out of nowhere—it took time, effort, and an awful lot of ingredients.

But this time, the bees and butterflies rallied around. While Lavender searched for enough dew to fill a buttercup, they flitted here and there among the lavender flowers, collecting the petals and pollen that their Flower Fairy friend needed to make her special soap. And so, for a second time, everything was washed and clean.

With so many creatures helping, it was finished in a twinkling. But things were not destined to run smoothly in the Flower Fairy Garden that afternoon. There were no drying lines. Not a single one.

The spiders' delicate gossamer strands had been snapped, tangled and ruined. What little was left wasn't big enough to hang a single fairy sock, never mind an entire Midsummer collection of clothes. The spiders had been frightened away by the commotion and no matter how softly or sweetly Lavender called, they were too scared to return.

"If you will allow me," said Periwinkle, bowing deeply in front of the forlorn fairy, "I will amaze you with the strong yet supple string I'll make from my flower stalks, which just happen to be perfect for washing lines. Are you watching . . . ?"

Lavender was watching. And she was definitely amazed.

29

The birds—who were quite a nosy bunch —had been watching all the frenzied fairy activity with interest. And when Rose and Honeysuckle began hanging string between the top stems of their plants, they could resist no longer. As one, they dived down to the garden to see what was going on.

"Perfect!" said Lavender, as the feathery creatures landed gracefully beside her. She'd soon realized that although Periwinkle was doing an admirable job, there was no way he could make enough washing lines to dry all the clothes before sundown.

"Here's what I'd like you to do," she said to the birds.

They looked at one another curiously and then looked back at the little Flower Fairy, who picked a dripping-wet petal tunic from the pile of clothes and handed it to the first bird. "Would you fly as high as you can and as fast as you dare until this is dry?" Lavender asked. "Please?"

The obliging bird nodded. And soon, the sky was fluttering with feathers and petals. It was a beautiful sight. Lavender paused for a moment to watch the whirl of color, then looked down, down, down at her checklist and heaved a great sigh.

Suddenly, the Midsummer Party seemed as far away as ever . . .

* * *

If Lavender thought she'd had a busy week, it was nothing compared to her hectic Friday afternoon. She'd never had so much to do or so many people to look after. And she'd never had so much fun. Gradually, she began to forget that anything had gone wrong at all.

She masterminded the whole project, flitting here and there to make sure everything was running smoothly. Tansy was repairing torn and shredded clothes, cleverly using petals and leaves to cover the ripped edges.

And no matter how closely Lavender looked, she was unable to spot where new petals had been sewn in place. Meanwhile, Iris was scrubbing extra hard at stubborn stains. Lavender skipped past, not forgetting to tell the hard-working fairy what a fine job she was doing, before helping to peg clean clothes on to Periwinkle's lines with bent twigs. Amongst the mayhem, she even managed to find a little time to make more fairy dust.

As the afternoon wore on, everyone began to tire.

"I'm pooped!" declared Periwinkle. He flopped down on a pillow of springy heather and mopped his brow. "I could easily go to … zzz …"

"Wake up!" said Lavender frantically. "There's still so much to do!" She tappety-tap-tapped Periwinkle's shoulder, until his eyes creaked open, but he immediately nodded off again.

31

"Can I help?" asked a singsong voice. It was Canterbury Bell—a blue-eyed fairy wearing a big purple hat, a pink shirt, and shorts made from the same silvery gossamer as his wings. He held a bunch of bell-shaped purple blossoms, which he swung to and fro so that they chimed loudly.

"Me too!" added Ragged Robin, a Flower Fairy whose tattered outfit lived up to his name, and who was not often seen in these parts—his home was the wet marsh outside the garden. "I heard about the unfortunate events and came as soon as I could," he explained. "I thought a Midsummer melody might cheer everyone up." And he played a lively tune on his reed pipe.

The beautiful fairy music wafted around the garden, lifting everyone's spirits at once.

The garden was bathed in the warm, rosy glow of the setting sun as the birds dropped the last of their dry clothes into Lavender's open arms.

"Thank you!" she called as they fluttered back to their nests and perches. And tired, but happy to have helped, the Flower Fairies returned to their homes to rest before the Midsummer Party.

Tomorrow, it would be time to have fun, but now it was time to sleep. Lavender returned to her cozy bed. Most of the dainty lilac flowers were gone now, but she knew that new buds would appear soon. She laid down her sleepy head, to dream of lovely fairy friends who'd been so kind.

Chapter Five
Party Time

The next morning dawned bright and clear. Soon the Flower Fairy Garden was filled with beautiful birdsong.

It was the perfect wake-up call. Lavender opened her eyes, then stretched luxuriously.

It was Midsummer's Day—the longest and most magical day of the year, and the day of the Midsummer Party. She could hardly wait!

Lavender fluttered from her snuggly bed of leaves down to the green grass below and splashed her face with drops of sparkling dew.

"Now I'm ready for anything!" she announced to a passing ladybird, who flapped her spotted wings in reply.

Gathering a few last stems of Lavender from her plant and bundling them under her arm, the little lilac fairy strode purposefully toward the piles of clean party clothes and the petals still drying on Periwinkle's washing lines. For the second time that week, she ran to and fro among the outfits, shaking her delicate flowers all about. A gentle breeze blew them here, there, and everywhere, until even the air was fragrant. A musical tinkling sound rushed through the garden, and suddenly there was magic in the air, too, making all the fairy petals sparkle and shine even more than the day before.

Carefully, Lavender began to pluck the clean clothes from the washing lines, marvelling again at how wonderful they looked. Soon, the pile was even taller than her!

Lavender gently placed Elder's delicate lacy dress into her waiting arms. "Ta-daaaa!" she said proudly. There was not a mud spot to be seen.

"Oh, Lavender . . ." breathed the little Flower Fairy, fluttering her pale, creamy wings. "This is wonderful . . . However can I thank you?"

Lavender blushed as she thought of all the fairies who'd lent a hand. "I should be thanking you," she said. "Just make sure that you have a marvelous time." And, staggering slightly under her load, she hurried to meet her next satisfied customer.

"Excellent!" said Honeysuckle, admiring the extra petals that had been sewn on to the bottom of his shorts, to make them super-tough.

"Superb!" said Periwinkle, whose blue tunic had been sprinkled with fairy dust to give it a silvery sheen.

Rose was so pleased with her dainty pink frock that she was speechless.

At twelve noon precisely, Canterbury Bell's flowers began to ring merrily. It was the sound that everyone had been waiting for—the signal that the Midsummer Party was about to begin!

Dressed in their finery, the Flower Fairies skipped and danced toward a clearing in a secret corner of the garden. This was the fairy court—where the very best parties in all of Flower Fairyopolis took place.

Ooohs and aaahs of delight echoed through the garden as the fairies saw the mouth watering fairy feast that awaited them.

There were fairy cheeses made from Mallow's delicious seeds, piles of ripe hazelnuts, bowls of wobbly crab-apple jelly, and nutshells filled to the brim with

34

Elderberry's fragrant juice. The Flower Fairies piled their daisy plates high with food and dipped buttercups into the purple juice.

And then the dancing started. Honeysuckle, Canterbury Bell, and Ragged Robin provided the music, while Columbine, Almond Blossom, and Fuchsia— who needed no excuse to whirl and waltz—led the way on to the dance floor.

Lavender gazed at the dazzling jumble of color before her eyes. Everything had turned out splendidly. And everyone looked wonderful. She was having the best time!

"Excuse me?"

She looked down as a tiny Sweet Pea fairy tapped her on the knee. "Yes, my sweet?" she asked.

"I have to give you this," said the tiny fairy solemnly, handing her a scroll of fairy parchment.

Lavender's heart dropped like a stone in a very deep well. She untied the golden strands coiled around the parchment and unrolled it, her stomach turning to jelly as she did so. She gulped. The message was from the Queen of the Meadow and Kingcup. They wanted to see her—at once.

Anxious thoughts chased around Lavender's head like nervous butterflies. The king and queen must be angry with her for creating mayhem in the peaceful garden. Would they banish her from the Flower Fairy Garden . . . ?

She went to find out.

Lavender tiptoed toward the King and Queen of the Flower Fairies, resplendent in their gorgeous royal robes. As she curtsied before them, she could not help but tremble.

"Why do you look so scared?" asked the Queen of the Meadow gently, her silky, golden hair glistening in the sunlight. She toyed with a string of olive-green pearls around her slender neck.

Lavender could not speak.

"We would like to thank you for your incredibly hard work," said Kingcup, a huge smile appearing on his handsome face. He looked around the assembled fairies, who were watching the meeting curiously. "At this time of year," he said, "Lavender becomes the most important fairy in the Flower Fairy Garden. Without her, the Midsummer Party clothes would be lackluster and dull and in some cases"—he winked at Honeysuckle—"quite dirty. But with Lavender's efforts, everyone dazzles."

"Er . . . Your Kingship, sir," said Lavender, unable to stay silent. "It's thanks to all the Flower Fairies that this Midsummer Party has turned out so well this year." She curtsied apologetically.

"That is a very noble thing to say," said the Queen of the Meadow. "But even so, your contribution has been quite magnificent. And I'm sure everyone would agree."

There were deafening cheers, and Lavender blushed. She didn't think she'd ever been so proud—or so happy.

Each Midsummer Party it was traditional to reward one of the Flower Fairies by singing their special song. This year, the honor belonged, of course, to Lavender. And everyone—from the smallest Flower Fairy to the regal Kingcup—gathered round to sing:

"Lavender's blue, dilly dilly"—so goes the song;
All round her bush, dilly dilly, butterflies throng;
(They love her well, dilly dilly, so do the bees;)
While she herself, dilly dilly, sways in the breeze!

"Lavender's blue, dilly dilly, Lavender's green;
She'll scent the clothes, dilly dilly, put away clean—
Clean from the wash, dilly dilly, hanky and sheet;
Lavender's spikes, dilly dilly, make them all sweet!"

The Song of
the Rose Fairy

Best and dearest flower that grows,
Perfect both to see and smell;
Words can never, never tell
Half the beauty of a Rose—
Buds that open to disclose
Fold on fold of purest white,
Lovely pink, or red that glows
Deep, sweet-scented. What delight
    To be Fairy of the Rose!

Rose's Special Secret

by Kay Woodward

Chapter One
A Narrow Escape

"I'll miss you," Rose whispered softly. The Flower Fairy looked at the tangle of thorns and withered leaves for the very last time. For as long as she could remember, this tatty, overgrown, *wonderful* rosebush had been her home. She'd trimmed and tended its crooked stems, encouraging the ancient plant to send out delicate pink buds every spring and summer. She'd done everything in her power to take care of it. And in return, the prickly plant had given her soft pink petals to wear and a beautiful place to live. But disaster was approaching— and not even fairy dust could save the rosebush now.

A loud *swoosh* interrupted Rose's melancholy thoughts, and she glanced up as a sparrow hurtled past, chirping noisily. When she heard what the anxious bird had to say, Rose hastily flung her leafy bag over one shoulder. *They* were on their way. It was time for *her* to go.

"Good-bye," said Rose, a lone tear trickling down her cheek. "I'll never forget you."

As if saying farewell, the rosebush waved in the breeze.

Feeling that her heart might break, the Flower Fairy gave a brief watery smile, took a deep breath, and then fluttered to the ground. She landed nimbly on dainty feet and hurried in the direction of the morning sun, which was already casting a golden glow over the leafy wilderness that lay before her. As she dodged around weeds and leaped over rocks, Rose's mind whirred.

It had been less than a week since the dreadful rumors had invaded the overgrown garden. The bees had started it, buzzing odd-sounding new words: *Decking. Concrete. Patio.* No one knew what they meant, but they sounded mean, dangerous, and very scary.

Then the human intruders came. They stomped through the garden, crushing delicate flowers and forging wide, muddy pathways with their enormous boots, even uprooting entire plants that had the misfortune to block their way.

Rose and her Flower Fairy friends could no longer hop and flutter freely from flower to flower—they now seemed to spend most of their time scurrying between one leafy plant and the next. They knew, as every Flower Fairy knows, that the only way to make sure that Flower Fairyopolis remained truly safe was by keeping it very, very secret. The only problem was, their precious homes were disappearing fast—and they were running out of places to hide.

"What are we going to *do*?" Rose cried helplessly to Dandelion. He was one of the toughest, most resourceful Flower Fairies she knew—as well as one of the most brightly dressed. If anyone knew how to deal with these troublesome humans, he would.

"*Do?* Oh, there's nothing we can *do*," Dandelion said matter-of-factly. He swung from one tall rose stem to another, his beautiful yellow-and-black wings almost dazzling Rose with their brilliance. "I've seen it all before. They come. They weed and rake and sow. They roll out carpets of green grass. And then they go. Before long, you have a lovely wilderness once more.'

"But where shall we *go*?" Rose said, her voice trembling. She was trying desperately not to cry, even though everything sounded pretty hopeless.

"It's all right for me," said Dandelion, smoothing down his jaunty yellow-and-green outfit. "It doesn't matter how many times they pull up my flower—it will always grow again. And I'm a bit of a wanderer at heart! But rosebushes . . ." He scratched his head, noticing for perhaps the first time that Rose didn't share his happy-go-lucky mood. "Well . . . if I were you, I'd take a holiday," he suggested kindly. "Go and see a bit of Flower Fairyopolis. Meet some new Flower Fairies. You might find another rosebush—one even better than this one."

"I'll *never* find a better home than this!" exclaimed Rose. But deep down, she knew that Dandelion was right. Her beloved rosebush wasn't safe any more—and no matter how much she disliked the idea of moving, she *had* to go.

Now, as she rushed toward safety, the tiny Flower Fairy thought she heard the distant sound of metal crunching into dry, cracked earth. Her steps quickened. In no time, she reached the crumbly bricks—covered with masses of pink and peach and lilac blooms—that marked the edge of the world she knew.

Rose looked up and up . . . and up. She'd been this way once before, but somehow, she didn't remember the wall being quite this high. It towered above her, the top so far away that it was almost out of sight.

Rose flopped down onto a nearby mushroom, resting the bag on her knee. Inside, she'd carefully stowed all her possessions: the petal dress that she kept for best, a sunny yellow flower that Dandelion had given her as a going-away present (he said that it would make an excellent

43

umbrella), a single pink rosebud to remind her of her old home, and a tiny gossamer bag of fairy dust. This last item had to be saved for emergencies. But as she peered up at the lofty wall, Rose realized that she would need all her fairy dust to help her fly over this—the very first obstacle that she'd encountered. Once her fairy dust was gone, what would she do *then* for fairy magic? She could make no more fairy dust until she found another rosebush.

"I say," said a soft voice, "you're looking terribly sad. Is there anything I can do to help?"

Rose brushed blonde curls from her eyes and examined the wall more closely. A Flower Fairy was watching her curiously from among gently ruffled pink petals. It was Sweet Pea! She wore a delicate pink skirt made from layers of the same petals as her flower, and a leaf-green bodice. Her hair was long, dark, and wavy.

"Because if you're wondering about climbing this wall, you needn't worry," Sweet Pea went on. "It's a snap. No need for even the tiniest pinch of fairy dust."

And Rose saw that it was true. The entire wall was covered with curly, green tendrils—ideal handholds and footholds for fairy feet. She grinned widely at the helpful Flower Fairy and picked up her bag once more.

"Come on," said Sweet Pea brightly. "I'll show you the way."

Chapter Two
Over the Wall

"Oooh . . ." breathed Rose. She'd never seen anything like it—ever. From her bird's-eye perch on top of the old wall, she gazed at a whole new world that stretched far into the distance. It looked utterly magical.

"Pretty good, eh?" said Sweet Pea. She sat peacefully beside Rose as she, too, admired the view.

Far below their fairy feet were flowers of every color and description. There were tall snapdragons, their plump yellow and red blossoms waving in the breeze. Billowing bushes of dusky lavender rustled to and fro, and ground ivy, speckled with tiny lilac flowers, crept along the moss-covered earth. Startlingly pink zinnia flowers stood proudly, while elegant yellow irises clustered along the banks of a sparkling stream.

"Where are we?" whispered Rose, noticing that Sweet Pea's pink, peach, and lilac flowers spread down this side of the wall, too.

"Why, this is the Flower Fairies' Garden," Sweet Pea announced proudly. "It's beautiful isn't it?"

Rose nodded wordlessly.

"You'll love it here," said Sweet Pea, suddenly distracted by a floaty dandelion seed that wafted past her nose. She peered down at the dandelion clock far below. "Goodness, is that the time?" She leaped to her feet and smoothed down her pink petticoats. "I'd better be going. You take care, won't you?" she added, flinging a leg back over the wall.

"Watch out for el—" she called as she disappeared.

"What?" Rose called after her. "Watch out for *what*?"

But Sweet Pea had vanished.

What could she have meant? thought Rose, worry crinkling her pretty forehead for a moment. Then she shrugged— it was probably nothing.

Another dandelion seed whirled past, giving Rose a splendid idea. She flipped open her bag and tugged out Dandelion's gift, admiring the tightly packed yellow petals. It would keep her dry in the rain, but it would catch the breeze too.

"One, two, three, fly!" cried Rose. Holding her dandelion aloft and clutching her bag, she leaped from the wall and soared through the air. Slowly, gracefully, the Flower Fairy swooped toward the garden, fluttering her pearly pink wings occasionally to change direction. As she approached the ground, her feet skimmed the topmost blossoms, releasing delicious, flowery scents. Lower, lower, lower she went, until—*thud!*—she landed on a cushion of springy moss.

Rose sighed with relief and looked around. All she could see were flowers—no Flower Fairies. Where were they?

46

"Well, hello!" sang a friendly voice. "Nice of you to drop in!" A mischievous face popped up from behind a bristly cornflower and skipped over. His entire outfit—jerkin, shorts, silken slippers, and even a crown —was pure, dazzling blue, made from the starry petals of his flower. "Welcome to the garden!" he added, bowing politely and waving a regal hand. "I'm Cornflower."

Rose clambered to her feet and bobbed a quick curtsey. "Pleased to meet you," she said, trying to ignore the warm blush that she could feel coloring her cheeks. She wasn't used to meeting strangers. "I'm Rose."

"Marvelous," said Cornflower. He looked quizzically at her, taking in the dishevelled clothes and ruffled blonde curls.

"I expect you'll want to get settled in," he said helpfully, bending to pick up her bag and dandelion. "Where's your flower?"

Her heart sank. Cornflower was being so kind, so helpful, so welcoming. She didn't know how to tell him that she didn't really belong here—that she didn't have a flower, not anymore. And she didn't even know if there *were* any rosebushes in the Flower Fairies' Garden for her to make her new home. What was she to *do?*

"I'm so sorry, my dear," said Cornflower. "Here I am, yabbering away. And there you are, worn out after your journey. In fact, I bet you're so tired that you can't remember *where* your flower is." He patted her shoulder sympathetically. "I'll help you find it."

"But—" began Rose.

"No buts!" said Cornflower, flinging Rose's bag over his shoulder and grasping the dandelion as if it were a floral spear. "Follow me!"

The eager fairy hopped and skipped merrily around the garden, while Rose hurried along in his wake. She tried once or twice more to explain why she was there, but it was no use. Cornflower simply said that there was no need to thank him, and that she should save her breath for the journey. Eventually, Rose did as she was told, scurrying to keep up with the sprightly Flower Fairy.

As they zigzagged between the flowers, the silent garden seemed magically to come alive. Beautifully camouflaged Flower Fairies popped out from behind blossoms, stems, and clumps of wild grass. They called out friendly greetings as the small procession passed.

Soon, Rose felt quite at home. "Everyone is *so* nice!" she exclaimed happily.

But there was no sign of a rosebush, not even a solitary rosebud. And meanwhile, the sun was moving unstoppably through the summer sky. By teatime, although they had searched most of the Flower Fairy Garden, they were still no closer to finding a place where Rose could lay her head. There remained just one place they hadn't explored.

"Why don't we try over there?" Rose asked, pointing to the dark, forbidding mass of undergrowth in the far corner of the garden.

"Oh, you won't find your rosebush in there," Cornflower said, shaking his head dismissively. "I think perhaps we'll try the area near the forget-me-nots again."

Rose hardly heard. She was far too busy pushing through the thick grasses that crowded in front of her, blocking her view. She weaved in and out of the tall, emerald blades until eventually she emerged at the other side. There, facing her, was a terribly overgrown thicket. And poking out of the very middle of the thicket—so tiny that most Flower Fairies would have mistaken it for a sharp twig—was a thorn.

A rose thorn.

Rose grinned from ear to ear. "I've found it!" she called happily.

"A rosebush?" said Cornflower, rustling through the grass to join her. "Really?" He peered uncertainly at the undergrowth. "It doesn't look very lived in," he added, looking at Rose as if thinking that she'd quite clearly gone mad.

"I'm sure," said Rose. "That's the place."

* * *

As the setting sun cast a rosy glow over the garden, Rose surveyed her new home. Cornflower had gone—reluctantly, and with a great deal of grumbling— after she'd persuaded him that she really would be absolutely, totally fine and that he wasn't to worry and that she would whistle loudly if even the tiniest thing was wrong. But now the light was fading fast and Rose realized that it was getting too dark to see anything at all, never mind explore.

She heard the gentle breathing of sleeping Flower Fairies echoing from nearby flowers and trees. The reassuring sound made her feel sleepy, and her eyelids began to droop. "I *am* feeling rather tired," she murmured to herself.

And using a fallen leaf as a coverlet, she snuggled down in a small grassy hollow. She soon drifted off to sleep. But her dreams were filled with strange mutterings.

Who is she? . . . I don't know! . . . What's she doing here? . . . Don't ask me! . . . Doesn't she know that we live here? . . . I don't know!

Chapter Three
Inside the Rosebush

Rose was awakened bright and early by the chirpy melody of the local lark.

"Morning!" she called out to the little bird. Then, cupping her hands around an acorn shell that had filled with dew during the night, she turned her attention to the overgrown thicket.

A dark, uninviting mass of gnarly stems reared up before her—dark and wild and spiky. Dried, crispy leaves had been blown into the bush by the wind. They plugged every gap, making it difficult to see far inside. Rose wasn't surprised that no one lived here. After thirstily draining the acorn cup, she set to work.

First she brushed away the old, crinkled leaves. Next she carefully pruned the outermost twigs by sprinkling a touch of fairy dust onto the stems, then nipping them between her fingertips. She couldn't help pausing to admire her handiwork every few moments—the bush was looking neater and healthier already. Better still, it was starting to look like a rosebush, instead of just a heap of tangled twigs. There was still no sign of any roses though.

Then came the exciting bit. Now that she'd cleared the edge of the plant, it was time to venture inside. With small spry steps, Rose made her way to the very heart of the rosebush,

51

pushing springy twigs and branches out of her path. It was farther than she had thought and, to make sure she didn't get lost, she left tiny sparkles of glittering fairy dust along the way. Little by little, the light grew dim and the sounds from the garden faded, while Rose grew more enthusiastic with every step. She was about to make a great discovery—she just *knew* it.

And then she did.

Suddenly, she burst through a particularly thorny patch to find that the sun was blazing down on the other side. And there, before her, was the loveliest sight she'd ever laid eyes on. In a small clearing grew a cluster of dainty rosebushes. All were in full bloom, their deep-red and soft pink flowers shining like jewels against the dark green leaves. There were tiny white rosebuds, too.

"A secret rose garden," breathed Rose. Was she the very first Flower Fairy ever to see this beautiful place? She *must* be. Otherwise, Cornflower would surely have known about it.

At once, her happiness was replaced by heartache. Rose was such a kindly soul that she couldn't bear the thought of these stunning flowers being hidden away where no one could see them. And then a thought pinged into her mind. *What if she were to clear a path through the outer bushes? Then the other Flower Fairies would be able to visit this marvelous place whenever they wanted—without having to battle their way through the spiky, dark undergrowth first.*

"Better still," she said aloud, "I could work some Flower Fairy magic on the overgrown rosebush too. With a little love and attention, it could look as

wonderful as my secret gar—!"

A sudden squawking noise interrupted her wonderful plan. Rose whipped her head around to see who had spoken, but there was not a creature in sight. When a large, glossy crow flew overhead and cawed loudly, she breathed a sigh of relief and chuckled to herself. Silly Rose! She was getting jumpy for no reason.

Briskly she spun on her heel, ducked into the undergrowth, and started back the way she'd come. And as she went, she made plans. She was going to turn her new home into a lovely place for everyone to enjoy. And she would only reveal the secret garden when all the hard work was done. That way, it would be a *real* surprise!

"Ouch!" Rose felt a sharp prickle, and her daydream vanished. She frowned and rubbed her leg. That wasn't supposed to happen—she was the Rose Flower Fairy! Rose thorns never pricked or poked her, not like they pricked and poked the other Flower Fairies who brushed against them.

Whether it was because she took care of roses and it was the plants' way of saying thank you, or whether she just had super-tough skin, Rose didn't know. The point was . . . she didn't *feel* pointy rose thorn things.

"Tee hee!"

Rose froze and darted quick glances to the left and right. That was no crow. It didn't sound like a Flower Fairy either. Someone was watching her—and laughing at her, too. She looked around frantically. Who could it be?

"That'll teach you to invade elf territory!" said a mocking voice.

Rose whirled to face a strange creature dressed entirely in green. He stood with his hands planted firmly on his hips, looking rather pleased with himself.

"Who are you?" she asked bravely.

The green-clad creature gave a short laugh and clicked his fingers. Instantly, two more creatures appeared, one on either side of him. They all stared insolently at Rose, and in the brief pause that followed, she couldn't help noticing how long and pointy their ears were. She also noticed that one of them was wielding a very sharp twig. So this was who had prodded her!

"*We*," said the leader importantly, "are the elves. And *we* live here."

"Pleased to meet you," said Rose. In a flash, she remembered Sweet Pea's words before she disappeared over the wall. She must have said, "Watch out for elves!" Rose didn't know much about elves, apart from their reputation for naughtiness and general mischief, but she was determined not to feel nervous.

"I live here, too," she added brightly. "I'm sure there's room enough for all of us."

"Ha!" barked the first elf. "But it's going to be no fun for us if you tidy everything up and make it all light and airy and *nice*." He said the last word as if it were a bad thing. "*We* like it dark and tangled. *We* are the elves."

"Yes," said Rose wearily. "You said." She tried
again, her sky blue eyes pleading with them to
understand. "The thing is, I'm Rose and it's my job
as a Flower Fairy to take care of this neglected old plant. I've
escaped from humans and decking and concrete and patios and
chaos to come here. My old home is about to be pruned, or worse."

"Chaos?" It appeared that of all Rose had said, the bossy elf
had heard just one word.

"Where is this place?" he demanded. "*We* like chaos.
We are th—"

"Yes, yes," said Rose hurriedly. "It's just over the wall
at the edge of the Flower Fairies' Garden."

The elves' dark, beady eyes glittered. As if triggered by
some unseen signal, the trio huddled together and spoke quickly
in low, excited voices. Then they faced Rose. "We've decided," said the leader
importantly. "You can keep your rosebush. *We're* going to make mischief."

Rose barely had time to nod before the three elves shot past her, the speed
of their departure spinning her around on the spot.
"Be nice to Dandelion, won't you?" she called
after them.

"What do you take us for?"
The indignant reply came from far away.
"We're not the pixies, you know!"

Laughing with relief, Rose followed her
glittering trail back through the overgrown
rosebush to the outside world. Now that
she'd solved the mystery of the muttering
voices and said good-bye to the twig-
wielding elves, she was free to get on with
what she did best—tending to rosebushes.

Chapter Four
A Magical Transformation

It was hard work, but Rose loved it. Politely refusing all offers of help, she spent her days pruning and trimming and neatening up the overgrown corner of the Flower Fairies' Garden. And whenever anyone asked for a guided tour, she simply flashed them a twinkly smile and tapped her nose. "Wait and see," was all she would say. Not even Cornflower's gentle teasing could entice her to reveal more.

Each evening, when she was tired—and very happy—Rose got to know the other Flower Fairies. They were very kind, inviting her to munch on tasty mallow seeds—a special sort of fairy cheese—and brewing her fresh cups of elderberry tea. While she ate and drank, different fairies entertained her with stories from the Flower Fairy Garden. Rose hadn't realized so many charming creatures lived there, and slowly she got to know each and every one. She was having a *marvelous* time.

The days went by. And, by the time the moon had grown from a thin, silvery sliver into a large shining ball and shrunk back to a sliver, Rose realized—with some surprise—that her work was nearly done. The overgrown corner of the garden had been utterly transformed. Gone were the long, tangled stems and withered leaves. In their place were healthy, young stems and fresh foliage.

Meanwhile, excitement in the garden had reached fever pitch. Although the Flower Fairies loved surprises, that didn't stop them from wondering endlessly what the hard-working fairy was up to. One day, Rose overheard two of the youngest Flower Fairies—White Clover and Heather—earnestly discussing the topic.

"I think she's practising circus tricks," said White Clover, a little fairy with round rosy cheeks. "She's learning to juggle with hazelnuts, where no one can see. That way, it's not embarrassing when she drops her nuts."

Heather wasn't convinced. "I think she's making rugs," he said knowledgeably. "She's collecting all of these old twigs so that she can weave them together. When Rose lets us inside the bush, we'll find that she's made a huge, twiggy carpet."

Rose covered her mouth to stifle a giggle, before hurrying away down the neat and tidy new path that she'd tunnelled through the rosebush. Little did the Flower Fairies know that not one but *two* surprises awaited them.

As well as tending the rosebushes, she had been busily collecting old petals to make rosewater. After collecting dew inside a large chestnut shell, Rose had added the petals to make a pink soup. Today, she was going to turn the soup into rosewater!

Carefully she climbed into the chestnut shell, which was wedged securely into a clump of moss to make sure that it didn't tip over. Lifting her left foot, then right, left, right, she squooshed and squished her toes into the water and petal mixture, turning it into a flowery mush.

"Mmmmm . . ." Rose sighed, as a beautiful smell began to drift upward. This rosewater would be the perfect way to thank the kind Flower Fairies for letting her stay in their garden. *Everything's ready*, she thought happily.

That evening, Rose hopped, skipped, and fluttered from flower to flower, inviting everyone to the far corner of the Flower Fairies' Garden the next day. Everyone was very excited, none more so than Cornflower, who regarded Rose as his special friend.

"Yes, yes," he said loudly to anyone who would listen. "It's all going to be a wonderful surprise, with lots of marvelousness and fabulous splendifery. You won't believe your eyes. Just wait and see!"

Honeysuckle, who was perched high on a curling tendril, grinned broadly. "You don't have a clue what's going on, do you?" he said, with a chuckle.

"Er . . . I . . . er . . . well, er . . . no," admitted Cornflower truthfully. "But I bet it's wonderful, all the same!"

He was right.

The next day dawned bright and clear, with not a cloud in the sapphire blue sky. Birds twittered cheerily from the branches of the silver birch tree. And the sun soon chased away the delicate wisps of mist that lingered near the ground.

Nervously smoothing down her best dress, Rose sat next to the rosebush that had once been so neglected and unloved. Now, it was a mass of green foliage. In the last day or two, tiny white-and-pink rosebuds had even begun to appear, like stars twinkling in a night sky.

Cornflower was the first to arrive. "All sorted?" he asked eagerly.

Rose nodded. There was something she needed to say—she just wasn't quite sure how to say it. Or how Cornflower would react. She took the plunge.

"The thing is, Cornflower . . . when we first met, I should have said that I didn't actually belong in the garden and that I didn't have a flower. It was just lucky that we found this rosebush—but, really, it's not mine." She didn't dare look up. "And I quite understand if you want me to leave the Flower Fairies' Garden, but I just want you to know that I love it here and—"

"Whoa there!" said Cornflower, flapping his gauzy blue wings. "Why did you think any of that would matter?" he asked, with a totally bemused expression. "We welcome all Flower Fairies into the garden, wherever in Flower Fairyopolis they come from." He raised a finger to his lips when Rose tried to speak. "Now, not another word! This is your home now."

She smiled gratefully.

Then, one by one, more Flower Fairies started to arrive, their faces bright with curiosity. There was Zinnia and Wild Cherry. Candytuft came next, then Lavender and Elder. Soon, everyone was there—the air buzzing with anticipation.

Rose clambered onto a toadstool so that she could see everyone. "I'd like to thank you all," she began quietly.

"Catch!" shouted Honeysuckle, throwing her one of his pinky-orange flowers. "Speak into that," he added. "Then we'll all be able to hear you!"

Rose smiled and put the trumpet-shaped flower to her lips. "You've made me so welcome," she went on. "So I'd like to welcome you to my secret garden. Except I don't want it to be a secret anymore. I want it to be a place for Flower Fairies to enjoy."

"Hurray!" shouted Cornflower.

"You've still no idea what's going on, have you?" Honeysuckle laughed.

"Nope!" said Cornflower, shrugging his shoulders. "But it's very exciting, all the same!"

"This way," said Rose, leaping down from her toadstool and tugging aside a large leaf that she'd positioned in front of the tunnel entrance. Then she stepped inside.

The way was leafy green and dappled with the sunlight that filtered through the rosebush. Rose had done so much pruning that the once dark and forbidding bush was light and airy. And the other Flower Fairies had no need to fear thorns—Rose had carefully twisted the stems so that the prickles pointed the other way. Ooohing and aaahing in wonder, they followed Rose deeper and deeper, until . . .

"*Wow!*" said Cornflower, as he emerged into daylight.

"*Amazing!*"

"*Unbelievable!*"

Exclamations of delight echoed around Rose's secret garden as the bedazzled Flower Fairies took in the view. Rose had nipped and shaped the dainty rosebushes until they were each a perfect ball. Any wilting flowers had been removed, leaving only the newest, freshest blooms. The large, dark red flowers looked as if their petals were made of velvet, while the pale pink and white rosebuds looked like soft marshmallows.

"And what's this?" asked Cornflower, dunking his finger into the chestnut shell. "Mmmm . . . That smells delicious!"

"It's rosewater," said Rose shyly. "Dab it on your wrists and behind your ears—you'll smell wonderful." She looked at the others. "It's for everyone to try," she said.

They didn't need telling twice. Soon the air was filled with the beautiful aroma of roses and the sound of happy Flower Fairies as they explored the new garden.

But for Rose, the very best part of the day didn't come until much later. She was relaxing happily among the leaves of the rose garden, thinking how much she loved her brand-new home, when she heard a pattering of tiny fairy feet. She peeped round a deep red rosebud to find Clover and Heather looking back at her.

"We've got a surprise for you," said Clover proudly.

"It's a poem," Heather chipped in.

"We wrote it," added Clover.

Then, before Rose had time to say a word, they began to recite the sweetest verse that she'd ever heard.

Best and dearest flower that grows,
Perfect both to see and smell;
Words can never, never tell
Half the beauty of a rose—
Buds that open to disclose
Fold on fold of purest white,
Lovely pink, or red that glows
Deep, sweet-scented. What delight
To be Fairy of the rose.

"I can't thank you enough," Rose breathed.

"Oh, don't mention it," said Clover, suddenly bashful. 'You've given us so much loveliness, we just wanted to give something to *you*.'

Chapter Five
A Surprise Visitor

For weeks afterwards, all anyone could talk about was the grand opening of the rose garden. It became an even more popular topic than the weather forecast—something that all Flower Fairies love to talk about. Gradually, the word spread beyond the garden to the marshland—a wet, grassy place that was teaming with dragonflies, minnows, and frogs. It was also the home of the Queen of the Meadow Fairy. Together with Kingcup, she ruled Flower Fairyopolis firmly yet fairly. She listened to the news of Rose's surprise with interest.

"I think perhaps that *I* should pay a visit to this garden," the queen mused aloud, her forehead puckered into a small frown. At once, she summoned a swallow and hopped onto its feathery back. "To the rose garden!" she commanded.

When the swallow swooped down into the middle of the inner rose garden, Rose was making herself a new party dress from pale- pink petals. She looked up in astonishment at the pretty Flower Fairy who slid gracefully to the ground.

A flaxen cloud of hair framed her delicate features. She was clad in a silken ivory-colored gown, and round her neck was a necklace of large, green pearls.

"I'm the Queen of the Meadow," said the fairy. She stretched out an elegant hand and grasped Rose's trembling fingers.

"P-p-pleased to meet you," stammered Rose, frantically scouring her mind for things that she might have done wrong. Otherwise, why would the queen of the whole of Flower Fairyopolis have bothered to come *here*?

"I'd like to look around," said the queen, her blue eyes sweeping left and right. "Would you show me your garden?"

"Why, of c-c-course, Your Royal F-Fairyness!" said Rose. At once, she realized what must be wrong. Obviously, the queen was cross with Rose for disturbing this corner of the garden. She must have preferred it when the roses were overgrown! But there was no sign of a royal telling-off—yet. The queen simply nodded, following Rose around the sculpted rosebushes.

64

And that was the exact moment the three elves chose to return from their travels. Giggling to themselves, they waited until the two Flower Fairies were out of sight before randomly plucking petals from the nearest bushes and scattering them on the ground.

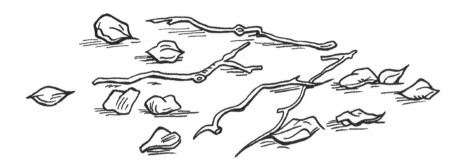

"Tee hee!" chuckled the elf in charge. "So messy!" His fellow elves nudged each other, then shook with silent laughter. When they heard voices approaching, they all hid.

"Oh!" gasped Rose, when she saw the torn petals. "I'm terribly sorry, Your Highness. The flowers are usually so neat. I don't know what happened."

The queen raised an eyebrow, but said nothing.

"I'll show you the secret tunnel," said Rose, desperate to impress the royal visitor, who she was sure must be seriously underwhelmed by now. She took Queen of the Meadow to the tunnel and led her inside.

"Pee-ew!" spluttered Rose. The tunnel smelt *awful*—as if a dozen bad eggs had been cracked there.

The queen wrinkled her nose in disapproval, but remained silent. The final straw came when she went to step back into the secret garden. A long stem suddenly shot out from the side of the tunnel, tripping her up. It was only the timely sprinkling of a little fairy dust that stopped Queen of the Meadow from sprawling on the grass.

"You can come out now," said the queen sternly, standing with her hands on her hips.

Rose popped her head out of the rosebush. "I'm sorry . . ." she began.

"No, not *you*," said the royal visitor tartly. Her arms were folded and she looked very cross. Suddenly, her voice softened and she pointed at three familiar figures who were now creeping out of the rosebush, their expressions sullen.

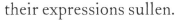

"*Them*."

"The elves!" exclaimed Rose.

"Well, what have you to say for yourselves?" said the queen, facing the mischievous trio.

The chief elf sighed dramatically. "*We* are the elves," he said petulantly. "*We* do mischief. That's our *job*."

"Then I suggest you do it somewhere else," replied Queen of the Meadow. "Rose has worked very hard to make this garden such a wonderful place. So unless you want to help with the pruning and weeding and tidying and . . ." She chuckled gaily as the elves spluttered in horror and sprinted back down the tunnel.

"*We* didn't like it here anyway!" they shouted. "It's too pretty!"

The queen turned to Rose, a wide smile revealing pearly white teeth. "Well done," she said. "I think you've done a marvelous job. This garden is magnificent. Of course, I knew all along it would be—I just wanted to come and admire it for myself." She clicked her fingers and the swallow soared back down to the garden, landing neatly beside her.

"Oh, thank you!" said Rose.

"Farewell!" called Queen of the Meadow. "Keep up the good work!"

Rose waved until her royal visitor was just a tiny speck in the distance. Then she settled down on a heap of moss and happily carried on with her sewing. She'd lost her old home, but now she'd found a wonderful new one and lots of fantastic Flower Fairy friends, too. Everything in her garden was truly rosy.

The Song of
the Strawberry Fairy

A flower for S!
Is Sunflower he?
He's handsome, yes,
But what of me?—

In my party suit
Of red and white,
And a gift of fruit
For the feast tonight:

Strawberries small
And wild and sweet,
For the Queen and all
Of her Court to eat!

Strawberry's New Friend

by Pippa Le Quesne

Chapter One
A New Friend

"Ouch!"

Strawberry pushed his way past the final bramble and emerged, very much the worse for wear, on the edge of a field.

"Ow, ow, ow!" he said, as he began to examine his injuries.

There were some painful scratches on his hands and arms and one knee was absolutely throbbing, but he was more worried about his wings. He'd been careful to fold them flat against his back as soon as he realized that what he'd taken for the perfect hiding place was, in fact, a tangle of brambles, but he could easily have torn them on the way through.

Although Flower Fairies can't fly that far, their delicate wings are very important to them: as part of their overall camouflage, for balance, and—of course—for flitting from plant to plant and up into trees to visit their friends. Cautiously, Strawberry opened his pair—which resembled pale green petals—and craned his neck round to investigate. They *looked* all right. He flapped them several times. *Yup, working nicely.*

Next, he straightened his floppy green sunhat and brushed the dirt off his matching red shirt and shorts. Then, feeling satisfied that all was in order, he sat down to attend to his knee.

A big rip in his right stocking revealed a nasty cut. When Strawberry had made sure that he was safely out of sight from the humans, he'd stopped in the middle of the bush and, gritting his teeth, pulled out a large splinter. It hurt a lot, but he was too angry to cry and besides, he couldn't afford to make any more noise having been lucky enough to get away with a yelp of pain already.

"That was *so* stupid," the little Flower Fairy said aloud.

Strawberry had been out exploring the lane when he'd stumbled across a handful of discarded cherry stones. He could never resist a game of fairy marbles and having hollowed out a pit with a stick and selected his shooter, he was soon absorbed in trying to knock the remaining stones into the hole. And because he was concentrating so hard on perfecting his shot, he didn't hear the children until they were almost upon him. So, by the time he'd come to his senses, he had to flee for the nearest cover—which, rather than being a nice safe hedgerow, had turned out to be a very prickly bush. The humans had passed by without noticing him, but Strawberry knew that he'd had a narrow escape and his heart was still thumping, not least because he'd broken one of the first Flower Fairy rules and let his guard slip.

"You could have been trampled on or . . . or . . . worse still, they might have actually seen you—and then what? Either you'd be imprisoned in one of those glass jar things by now or they'd be searching high and low for the rest of the Flower Fairies and that would all be YOUR FAULT!" Strawberry continued to scold himself as he pulled a handkerchief out of the pocket of his shorts, folded it lengthways and attempted to tie it round his leg.

Just then, he heard what sounded like a giggle and, dropping the makeshift bandage, he jumped to his feet. "Who's there?" he said, looking about but not seeing anyone.

This time there was a snort of laughter—and it came, quite clearly, from the bramble bush. Ignoring the pain in his knee, Strawberry spun round and stood with his hands on his hips.

"Show yourself!" he demanded—feeling rather indignant that someone should be laughing at his obvious discomfort.

"I'm not hiding from you, you know," said a voice. "I'm right in front of your nose."

Not quite believing that anyone would be in among the prickles out of choice, Strawberry moved closer to the bush, being careful not to catch himself on any of the harmful canes. And there, sitting casually *astride* one of the branches, was another Flower Fairy!

Strawberry was somewhat taken aback and stood staring at her for a moment or two. She had lovely opaque wings that complimented her soft pink petal skirt and deep purple tank top. She was grinning at him playfully and he could see immediately that she hadn't meant to be unkind. But what was most surprising was that her legs and arms were quite bare and completely without a single scratch.

"Boo!" the Flower Fairy said suddenly, bringing Strawberry to his senses.

"Sorry—I didn't mean to stare—but . . . but . . . how come . . ."

"How come the thorns don't hurt me?" Finishing his sentence for him, she leapt out of the bush and landed lightly on the ground beside him. "Because it's a blackberry bush and it's my plant so I'm protected," she explained, drawing his attention to the pinkish-white flowers that peeped out of the brambles. Each one had five flat petals and a center made up of lots of hairy yellow stamen—not dissimilar to Strawberry's own flowers.

"Ah," he said, "so you're Blackberry. I think we might be second cousins, you know."

"I think you're right," Blackberry replied. "It's Strawberry, isn't it?" Then without giving him a moment to reply, she linked her arm in his. "I'm terribly sorry about your knee. Listen, we'll go and visit Self-Heal and she'll patch you up and then perhaps we can come back here for a cup of my special tea or a game of hopscotch? Oh, but your knee probably hurts too much for that . . ."

And after stuffing his handkerchief into her own pocket, she led him off down the field, chatting away cheerfully as though they'd been friends forever.

Chapter Two
Happy Days

"Look out—here I come!"

Blackberry, clinging on to a bouncy weeping willow branch, sprang off the grassy verge and swung out across the pool, dipping her toes into the cool water and whooping with delight as she went.

Strawberry was sitting on the opposite bank, tugging off his socks and shoes. He grinned at his friend as she gathered momentum and soared back and forth through the air.

It had been a couple of weeks now since she had taken him to have his knee bathed and bound by Self-Heal and, in that time, not only had the cut completely healed, but he and Blackberry had become inseparable. It turned out that they had loads in common—they both liked playing marbles and hopscotch, teaching the baby Flower Fairies to roll and crawl, eating Candytuft's delicious fairy fudge— and basically anything else that involved having fun. Sometimes they just lay on their backs for hours in the open fields watching larks swooping or clouds skudding across the sky, talking about all the things they'd like to do and see together. And they were constantly finding new ways to make each other laugh.

"Here I go!" Strawberry shouted, grabbing a branch and taking a running jump to launch himself across the pool.

Blackberry had almost come to a standstill, enjoying the sensation of gently swaying with the tree as its branches skimmed across the water. As he passed her by, Strawberry suddenly had an idea. "Watch this," he called. And then taking hold of the branch above his head, he began shinnying up it until he'd disappeared into the thick canopy of leaves. Then, bringing his knees up to his chest, he let go of the willow and dive bombed into the lagoon below.

* * *

"There's one!" exclaimed Blackberry, pointing at the fish that darted out of the shadows. It was small with a dark back, golden belly and sides, and beautiful bright red fins.

The two Flower Fairies were lying on the bank on their tummies—minnow-spotting. It was the time of year when male minnows' scales transformed from dull green and black into spectacular colors.

Strawberry loved watching the lively little fish and it was ideal for passing the time while they dried off in the heat of the afternoon sun. Blackberry, every bit as daring as her friend, had jumped straight in after him and soon they were clambering in and out of the pool, splashing about and shrieking with laughter, not stopping until they had thoroughly exhausted themselves.

Now, they were so engrossed in their current activity that they didn't notice Willow alight on the grass beside them. She'd been at the fairy market all morning and so this was the first she'd seen of the companions.

"You two are like peas in a pod!" she exclaimed, gazing at their reflections in the water, which acted as a mirror now that the ripples had vanished along with the minnow. It was true—both Strawberry and Blackberry had curly dark hair and heart-shaped faces with plump rosy cheeks. Not only were their personalities similar but they looked alike too!

They turned round at once and smiled up at the pretty Flower Fairy. She had long wavy honey-blonde hair and she wore a lovely dress made from the elegant leaves from her tree and stitched with a red ribbon. Her wings were narrow and elongated and almost identical to those of a dragonfly.

"Willow—we've had such a great time swinging from your branches and swimming in the pool!" Blackberry gushed.

"I'm so glad." Willow raised an eyebrow but smiled kindly. "Listen—I've got some warm seed cakes in my basket. You must be ravenous after all that exercise—why don't you join me for tea?"

"Oh, I'd love to—thanks," said Strawberry, 'but it's time I was getting back. The humans have got a new kitten and he's causing havoc in the flower beds—so a garden meeting has been called. Another time, though." Unwillingly, he got to his feet and prepared to set off. The smell of Willow's freshly-baked cakes was making his mouth water.

"Here you are—one for the road!" Willow laughed as she reached into her basket and handed him a warm little package.

Strawberry grinned and waved goodbye to them both, before heading off towards the Flower Fairies' Garden and his own special patch, munching happily as he walked.

"Meet me after breakfast in the usual place," Blackberry called after him. Strawberry waved an arm in the air in response. Then, swallowing the last delicious mouthful of honey-coated seeds, he sighed contentedly to himself. Life was good.

Chapter Three
A Revelation

Strawberry shifted impatiently from foot to foot. He was waiting for Blackberry on the lane-side of the garden wall, just as he had done every day for the past fortnight. But today was different. When he'd opened his eyes first thing that morning, he'd been greeted by a very exciting sight. Now he was bursting to tell his friend the news.

It was the first week of June and summer was well under way. Each day felt hotter than the previous one and as the sun seemed reluctant to go to bed, the evenings were gloriously long. This was when strawberry plants everywhere produced yellowy-green heart-shaped fruit that ripened into soft, juicy, red berries. And for Strawberry, this meant that he'd be hard at work on his patch during the course of the next couple of months.

All the Flower Fairies loved his fruit, but not least Queen of the Meadow— and so whenever he wasn't busy harvesting the berries and carefully storing them, Strawberry would make special trips to the marsh to deliver the pick of the crop to the royal court. It was an industrious period and didn't leave much time for fun, but Strawberry—like all the Flower Fairies—got an enormous amount of pleasure out of tending his plants.

He was just thinking about how he would make an extra-large batch of jam this year and give some to all of his friends, including Blackberry, when a familiar voice broke into his thoughts.

"Morning!"

It was Blackberry, at last, skipping down the lane towards him.

"You look very perky—what have you got planned for today?" she asked.

"Hopefully the same as you," Strawberry replied.

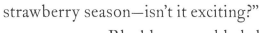

Then, not able to hold it in any longer, he blurted out, "My first batch of berries has ripened! It's officially the start of the strawberry season—isn't it exciting?"

Blackberry nodded slowly. "Er . . . yes," she said, rather half-heartedly. "But doesn't that mean you've got to spend the day looking after them?"

"Well, yes, of course!" Strawberry looked slightly confused. "But I've worked it all out. Presumably yours are ripe too—or nearly there? And so we can help each other out and still spend loads of time together. It'll be brilliant."

He grinned broadly at his friend, expecting her to be bubbling over with excitement too. Instead, he couldn't help noticing that she looked really quite sad. "What on earth is the matter?" he asked her.

79

"Oh, Strawberry—didn't you know—blackberries aren't ripe until August at the earliest. They're an autumnal fruit, not a summer fruit." And with that, a single tear slid down her cheek.

The little Garden Fairy's face fell. He couldn't believe his ears. "But ... but ... I thought *everything* about us was the same."

"So did I," Blackberry responded, sniffing noisily.

They stood in silence for a moment or two, neither of them knowing what to do. Then, all of a sudden, Blackberry said, "This is ridiculous! You're my dearest friend and you always will be and we're not going to let something as silly as this get in the way." She rubbed her eyes furiously and put on her best smile. "Listen—I'm not going to be busy and so there's no reason why I can't come and help you out each day. And then you can come and help me when it's my fruit's turn. It'll be perfect!"

"I hadn't thought of that ..." Strawberry murmured, immediately feeling much better. He reached over and patted her arm appreciatively. "Well, if you're sure?"

Blackberry nodded enthusiastically.

"Great!" Strawberry said, turning in the direction of the old stone wall. "Come and have a look then and we can decide where to start." And beckoning for her to follow, he found himself a hand-hold and began to hoist himself up.

"That should do it." Strawberry said, crawling backwards out from under one of his plants.

He'd been busy placing wet straw all around the patch so that the fruit wouldn't dry out, and he was pleased to have completed the task before the afternoon sun set in. Glancing up at his friend, he noticed that she looked hot and a little upset.

It was a week now since Blackberry had promised to come and help him each day and she had been as good as her word. She had worked hard alongside him, but now Strawberry could tell that the adventurous Flower Fairy was getting bored.

"I tell you what—let's go for a swim," he suggested suddenly.

"Really?" said Blackberry, brightening up, "but didn't you want to gather a basket of berries today for Queen of the Meadow?"

"It can wait and I could do with a break," Strawberry replied cheerfully. "Besides, when it's this hot, they spoil quickly if you pick them."

"Let's go, then," Blackberry said eagerly. "Race you to the willow pond!"

* * *

"... five, four, three, two, ONE. Ready or not, here I come!" Strawberry shouted.

The two Flower Fairies were playing a game of hide-and-seek on their way back to the garden. The refreshingly cool water had been the perfect remedy and it was great to spend some time together, having fun.

"I bet she's hiding somewhere in my patch," Strawberry said to himself. "I'll be as quiet as I can and creep up on her." He chuckled to himself as he took off. They'd just scrambled over the wall, so it wasn't far to fly now, plus approaching from the air would give him a better view. But he'd only flown a short distance and hadn't even begun searching for his friend, when he heard what sounded like a wail of misery. His stomach lurched—if he wasn't mistaken, it had come from his corner of the garden. Beating his wings as hard as he could, he headed straight for the strawberry patch.

Sure enough, standing there and wringing her hands was Blackberry. She was staring ahead with an expression of utter dismay. "Oh goodness! Oh goodness!" she was saying over and over again. And when Strawberry followed her gaze, his heart sank right down into his shoes.

It was the most awful scene that he had ever laid eyes on: for strewn all over the place were strands of straw, tattered leaves and squashed berries.

Chapter Four
From Bad to Worse

During the course of the last three days, Strawberry had finally got his patch back in order and a new crop of berries was already ripening. Lots of the Flower Fairies had stopped by to offer their help, bringing him lemonade or something to eat. But he was still feeling miserable.

Everyone agreed that it must have been the kitten who'd made such a mess. Yet no one had been able to come up with a satisfactory solution. So Strawberry had spent every waking minute guarding his plot and, at night, in order to catch a few hours' sleep, he'd liberally sprinkled fairy dust over the plants to cast a spell that would protect them. But his supplies were running low and there was no time to grind up pollen to make some more. Besides, it wasn't a long-term answer to the problem—for him or any of the Garden Fairies.

However, what was bothering him most of all was that he had barely seen Blackberry since the catastrophe had happened. She'd been so helpful at the time, finding other fairies to help clean up, and fetching a cup of calming camomile tea. She'd even offered to keep watch for the night so that he could get some sleep. But since then she'd only stopped by once and that was just a fleeting visit.

Strawberry blamed himself—
she'd been in the middle of telling
him a joke, when he'd snapped
at her and told her that he was
busy. And now he felt guilty
because she was just being
her usual bubbly self and
couldn't know that he didn't
feel like laughing. More than
that, he missed her. Their last
swim together felt like a distant memory now.

The little Flower Fairy was standing in between a row
of plants, all of this going through his mind and causing his forehead to wrinkle
with concern, when a voice called out.

"Hello there, Strawberry! You'd better watch out or the wind might change
and your face will be stuck like that forever!"

It was Herb Robert, grinning at him
cheekily. He was a friendly fairy and
Strawberry was always pleased to see him.
His tiny flower made its home in the nooks
and crannies of the wall that bordered the
lane, and he was often popping over either
to visit his cousin, Geranium, or to catch
up on the garden gossip.

"So I hear that all is not well in the Flower
Fairies' Garden," Herb Robert said. He was not
much taller than Strawberry but his appearance
was quite different. He had an angular face with
very pointed ears and his wings were those of a
brown and pink patterned butterfly.

"Blackberry told me all about it," he went on. "You know, you should go and see Self-Heal—she's full of good ideas. I bet she'd know what to do about this kitten."

Strawberry didn't fully take in this last part—his ears had pricked up at the mention of his friend. "You've been talking to Blackberry? How is she?"

"Well, you'll soon see for yourself," replied Herb Robert. "I believe she's coming to visit you this afternoon. Anyway, I've got to be on my way. Geranium's expecting me for lunch, so I'd better not be late." And without further ado, he waved goodbye and strode off in the direction of the flowerbeds.

* * *

Strawberry was surprised at just how nervous he felt. Once he'd finished watering his plants and had checked that the kitten wasn't nearby, he set about straightening himself up.

He was just pulling on a clean pair of shoes when a hand came out of nowhere and covered his eyes. Then a chirpy voice said, "Guess who?"

"Blackberry!" he exclaimed, his heart lifting for the first time in days.

"Yes, it's me!" she replied, removing her hand from his face.

Strawberry eagerly spun round to greet her. But when he saw that Blackberry hadn't come alone, a huge wave of disappointment washed over him. Next to her stood a slender Flower Fairy dressed in a burgundy and maroon tunic, with gossamer pink wings and a

headdress of round purple berries.

"This is Elderberry," his friend said. Strawberry nodded a hello.

"She lives near me and we met the other day," babbled Blackberry. "We had such an adventure—"

"Aren't your berries ripe yet either?" Strawberry butted in, addressing the newcomer rather abruptly.

"No, no. My fruit is autumnal." Elderberry smiled sweetly. "These ones are dried," she added, touching the crown of berries nestling in her hair.

"Oh," said Strawberry, glancing down, not able to look either of them in the face.

He knew that he should apologize to Blackberry for rudely interrupting her. And he was well aware that he was behaving badly and quite unlike himself.

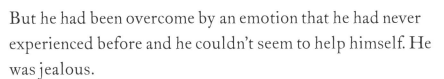

But he had been overcome by an emotion that he had never experienced before and he couldn't seem to help himself. He was jealous.

"Well," said Blackberry, after a moment in which no one had spoken, "Er—I can see that you're busy, so we'll leave you to it."

Strawberry continued to stare at his shoes. There was a gnawing feeling in the pit of his stomach and he felt sick.

"I'll see you—soon?" she added then turned to go, followed by Elderberry, who was obviously puzzled by the friends' odd behavior.

"Bye," Strawberry whispered as he watched the two fairies go flitting off back toward the garden wall.

He stood in the same spot until they were out of sight and then threw himself down to the ground and buried his head in his arms.
If he'd been miserable before Blackberry's visit, now he was really wretched.

Chapter Five

Some Wise Words

Of all the Flower Fairies, Self-Heal most resembled a human. Obviously she had wings; she was less than four inches tall and, like many of her friends, pinned her hair back on either side with one of her flowers. But her clothes were more conventional than the other fairies'—she wore an apron over a dress with a waist and puff sleeves, and she had a maternal way about her. More than that, she seemed to possess knowledge outside the ordinary realms of Flower Fairyopolis.

As well as taking care of her own kind, she helped and healed many creatures from the animal kingdom, and even the naughty elves were known to stop by for a cure or some advice. When Strawberry couldn't bear to dwell on his dreadful encounter with Blackberry any more, he had set his mind to resolving the kitten problem and it was then that Herb Robert's words had popped into his head: *you should go and see Self-Heal— she's full of good ideas.*

So now he was perched on a mushroom stool in the shady corner of the meadow where Self-Heal lived, watching her bind a field mouse's paw. It struck him that it was quite a novelty these days, to be sitting down and relaxing. Feeling confident that Tulip would be keeping a close eye on his patch, Strawberry cleared his thoughts and enjoyed listening to the little mouse as he chattered away to Self-Heal. "There we are," the gentle Flower Fairy said eventually, as she tied a double-bow to secure the bandage and patted her patient on the head. "Come back in a couple of days and I'll see how it's doing."

After the mouse had squeaked his goodbye and she'd watched him hobble off through the long grass, Self-Heal turned to Strawberry. "Well, I don't know about you," she said, "but I'd love a cup of tea!"

Strawberry sighed and then took a large thirst-quenching mouthful of mint tea. He had been talking for a long time now and although nothing had changed, he somehow felt different. He had only intended to tell Self-Heal about the kitten problem but when she had asked him to start from the beginning, he found himself relaying all the events of the last month— from when he had first met Blackberry, to earlier that afternoon when he had been so rude to her.

Self-Heal had looked very thoughtful all the way through his story and then, without saying a word, she'd sprung to her feet and begun rifling through her walnut chest.

"Here we are—I've got just the thing." She held out a small packet for Strawberry to take. "Careful how you open it," she added.

Laying it flat on the ground, he slowly unfolded the beech leaf to reveal a heap of miniscule seeds. "What are these?" he asked curiously.

"Catmint seeds!" Self-Heal replied. "Mix them with some fairy dust to make them grow quickly and sprinkle them all over the Flower Fairies' Garden. It's very important that you choose spots away from everyone's plants to sow them, but I guarantee that before you know it, that kitten won't be causing any more trouble."

"Well, that would be marvelous," said Strawberry, "but how does it work?"

"It's a type of mint that cats can't resist— hence its name," the knowledgeable Flower Fairy explained. "You just watch that kitten of yours. He'll be so busy rubbing up against it, licking and chewing the leaves and purring contentedly that he won't be in the slightest bit interested in anything else in the garden."

"How amazing!" Strawberry exclaimed. "Oh, Self-Heal, you're incredible." And quite forgetting himself, he ran over and gave her an enormous hug.

Self-Heal laughed and then holding the little Garden Fairy at arm's length, she looked at him seriously. "As for your other problem—the only way to solve that is to do some growing *yourself*."

"What do you mean?" Strawberry was confused.

"You have to realize that just because Blackberry has other good friends, it doesn't change how she feels about you. In fact, it's a good thing." She paused for a moment. "It's great when you have lots in common with someone, but differences are important too and so is time apart. It all enriches your friendship and means that the time you have together is even more special. Do you understand?"

"I think so," Strawberry said slowly. It was a lot to think about.

"Good," Self-Heal said, her lovely face breaking into an enormous smile. "Now, run along—you've got some gardening to do!"

* * *

"Fairy dust, fairy dust, make these plants grow—help them spread evenly and not at all slow!" Strawberry spoke softly, repeating the rhyme as he stirred the special mixture with his forefinger.

Then, taking a good-sized pinch, he flung it out across the lawn. At first, it looked as though the seeds were going to plummet down and land in the grass, which would have been disastrous. But then the tiny particles began to glimmer and sparkle and gradually they separated before whizzing off in various directions and vanishing from sight as they nestled into the earth.

"Right," said Strawberry. "With a little bit of luck, that will have done the trick. Now, I'd better let Tulip know that I'm back and see if I can persuade her to do another shift for me tomorrow morning, Although goodness knows if Blackberry will ever want to talk to me again . . ."

Chapter Six

A Big Surprise

Blackberry was standing on the path next to Elderberry, their heads together as if the two of them were carefully examining something. They looked so at ease with one another that Strawberry couldn't help feeling a pang of jealousy.

"Now," he said under his breath, "remember everything that Self-Heal told you." He took a moment to reflect on her wise words and remind himself how much sense they'd made when he'd mulled them over on the way home. And as he was thinking about all of this, a terrible notion came into his head . . . If he didn't stop being jealous and start behaving like a proper Flower Fairy, then Blackberry might not want to be friends with him at all. He gulped. That would be just too awful.

So, taking a deep breath, he leaned over and tapped his friend on the shoulder.

Blackberry turned her head and, although it was just for a second, Strawberry distinctly saw her eyes light up. His heart filled with hope.

"Hello." He cleared his throat. "I've come to apologize."

"Apologize?" Blackberry repeated the word, as if she couldn't quite believe her ears.

"Yes," Strawberry replied sheepishly.

By now, Blackberry was on her feet. She shot her friend a glance and Elderberry nodded ever so slightly before disappearing into the meadow grass, stooping to pick up a long thin object on her way.

The two remaining Flower Fairies stood facing one another, both feeling awkward and neither of them speaking for a moment or two.

"I'm sorry!" Strawberry said suddenly.

"So am I," chimed in Blackberry. "But you go first." She smiled at him, which was enough to give him all the encouragement that he needed.

"It's like this . . ." And Strawberry went on to explain that he'd only been so unpleasant because he'd missed her so much—and, so, when she did turn up but with another friend, it had made him feel horribly jealous.

Blackberry let out a giggle.

"What's so funny?" he asked, slightly hurt.

"Oh, I'm just so relieved," she said. "I thought you were acting like that because you blamed me for all those plants being destroyed."

"What?" Strawberry replied, as it dawned on him what a huge misunderstanding the whole thing had been.

"Well, I know that you only suggested going for a swim to be nice, and that if it wasn't for me, you'd never have left your patch that day. Besides, when I came back to see you the next morning, you snapped at me." She raised her eyebrows at him as if to emphasize her point.

"Oh, Blackberry. Don't be ridiculous. I was just upset because there was so much work to do. I really am sorry."

"That's OK!" She caught him round the neck and planted a big kiss on his cheek. "It's so good to see you again!"

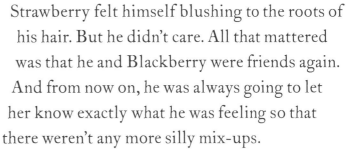

Strawberry felt himself blushing to the roots of his hair. But he didn't care. All that mattered was that he and Blackberry were friends again. And from now on, he was always going to let her know exactly what he was feeling so that there weren't any more silly mix-ups.

* * *

All around the garden small, dense plants with mauve-colored flowers had sprung up overnight, and the kitten couldn't get enough of them.

"Self-Heal is so clever, isn't she?" commented Blackberry to her two friends.

"I know, it's incredible," replied Strawberry, as he watched the cat take another swipe at a clump and then roll over on to the grass with pleasure.

"It must be such a relief for you all," Elderberry said kindly, as she rose to her feet.

The Garden Fairy nodded in response. It was true—it would mean that he wouldn't have to be tied to his patch all the time and could afford to enjoy himself a bit. "Are you leaving already?" he asked.

"Yes. I said I'd drop in on Rose while I was here." The elegant Flower Fairy opened her wings in preparation. Then, reaching into the bag at her side, she pulled out a familiar-looking object and held it out to Strawberry. "This is for you," she said.

He had only caught a glimpse of it in the meadow, but he knew it was the thing that she had picked up before she'd left him and Blackberry to talk. It was a whistle!

"It's made from a stem from my tree. From what I've seen they play quite well!" Elderberry chuckled.

Strawberry was speechless. Then he said solemnly, "I don't really deserve this—but thank you very much. It's wonderful." He beamed at the Tree Fairy, who winked to show him there were no hard feelings. She tousled Blackberry's hair affectionately, and then flew off in the direction of the rose garden.

"That was the adventure I tried to tell you about before you were so rude," Blackberry said, digging her friend playfully in the ribs, before she went on. "We spied some boys making them one day. They bored holes in the hollowed-out stems and then played them just like whistles. We thought it might be a nice thing for you to do at the end of a hard day's work."

"Well, you're very thoughtful." Strawberry blushed with pleasure. "And listen—I'll get Ragged Robin to teach me. He's really good at the pipes and I know you'll like him."

As he had this idea, he was struck by the realization that both he and Blackberry were going to benefit greatly from the fact that their fruit ripened at different times of year. He could get to know her autumnal friends and she could meet the Flower Fairies whose plants were in season at the same time as his.

"I'll come and play for you and Elderberry while you're busy harvesting,' he added, thinking out loud.

"Great!" said Blackberry enthusiastically. 'And don't forget that we'll still have two whole seasons to look forward to when neither of us will be working. We can spend all the time in the world together then. You'll be quite sick of me by the end of next spring!'

"Never!" Strawberry replied.

And he meant it. He knew that he couldn't possibly tire of his outgoing, brilliant companion, but that, also, he'd never let jealousy get in the way of their friendship ever again. Life was too short and there were far too many adventures to be shared!

The Song of
the Candytuft Fairy

Why am I "Candytuft"?
That I don't know!
Maybe the fairies
First called me so;
Maybe the children,
Just for a joke;
(I'm in the gardens
Of most little folk).

Look at my clusters!
See how they grow:
Some pink or purple,
Some white as snow;
Petals uneven,
Big ones and small;
Not very tufty—
No candy at all!

Candytuft's Enchanting Treats

by Kay Woodward

Chapter One
Fairy Friendship Week

"You're totally sure?" Candytuft said earnestly. "I mean, it would be completely wonderful if you did, but I wouldn't want you to go to any trouble—"

"I really think you ought to take a breath now," said Lavender with a giggle. "Honestly, it would be my pleasure. It is Fairy Friendship Week, after all."

Of course! A wonderfully warm feeling rushed from Candytuft's dainty toes to the tips of her pearly pink wings and back again. Of all the festivals and parties held each year in Flower Fairyopolis—and there were quite a lot of these, because fairies just *love* special occasions—this had to be her absolute favorite.

Fairy Friendship Week was a time for fairies to spoil each other silly, with treats and surprises galore. If Flower Fairies could think of an extra-special way to cheer up a friend, they would. If they could help out with the dullest tasks to brighten a fairy's day, they'd do that too. And this was precisely why Lavender had offered to do Candytuft's laundry.

"This is ever so kind of you," said Candytuft, scrambling frantically below the white, pink and purple blossoms of her flower. "However hard I scrub my clothes, they never look as spick and span as when you do it. And how do you make them smell so beautiful? *Aha!*"

Triumphantly, she waved a pair of shorts and a sleeveless tunic—made from the most delicate of petals—in the air, before diving back beneath the plant again.

"The secret is in my special soap," said Lavender brightly. She scooped up the purple petals and admired them. "And a sprinkling of fairy magic, of course," she added quietly to herself.

Candytuft's leaves trembled alarmingly as the little fairy searched among the stems. At last, she found what she was looking for.

"Ta-daaa!" she announced, bringing out a small pile of white petals. "Handkerchiefs!" she explained. "Ooops—here are more!" She spied another heap of white petals lying beside her cooking pot and gave everything to Lavender. "That's everything!" she said cheerfully.

"Now, are you *really* sure you don't mind?"

"Not at all," said Lavender, looking genuinely delighted at the prospect of sinking her arms into a tub of soapy suds. "That's what friends are for." And she fluttered away in the direction of the stream.

Candytuft waved goodbye, then rubbed her hands together delightedly. Now it was her turn. And although she might be terrible at laundry, she was an absolute whiz at making candy. And luckily, she'd made huge batches of her two most popular treats just the week before. She had more than enough Snapdragon Sherberts and Marigold Mallows to treat the whole of Flower Fairyopolis.

"Excellent," said Candytuft briskly to herself. Perhaps she could wrap the treats with her leaves and decorate each package with a tiny flower . . . That really would look lovely. She thought of her friends' faces when she presented them with her gifts—they were sure to be thrilled.

"Now, where is that candy?" muttered Candytuft, whose other great talent was talking. She was so chatty that she'd talk to anyone and everyone about anything and everything. The weather . . . the latest fairy fashions . . . which shoots were peeping through the soil . . . who the handsome Kingcup might dance with at the Midsummer Party . . . She would talk to whoever would listen, whether they were a Flower Fairy, a bird or a bee. And if there wasn't a soul nearby, then Candytuft would simply talk to herself. She was a very good audience.

The pretty fairy hopped lightly about the flower bed where her plant grew, using her gossamer wings to lift her a little higher. Like the other Garden Flower Fairies, Candytuft didn't fly long distances. She walked, skipped or hopped as much as she could, tending only to take to the air when she wanted to reach a tree, or even just for fun. If she had to travel further afield, she would hitch a lift with an obliging bird or a dragonfly.

"I'm sure I left them here," Candytuft told a passing wasp.

It buzzed helpfully in reply, nosing gently around the clusters of pretty pink, white and purple blossoms.

"Oh no . . ." said Candytuft. It all came flooding back. Last weekend, she'd happily handed over her entire candy supplies to the Midsummer Party committee. Every last treat. So she had nothing to give her fairy friends this week. "What shall I do?" she cried.

The wasp buzzed in her ear. And then it buzzed away.

Candytuft sighed and shook her head. The wasp was right. There was only one solution— and that was to make more candy for her friends. It would mean quite a lot of hard work, but if she stirred and mixed like crazy, she might have just enough time to create some wonderful treats for Fairy Friendship Week.

It was not in Candytuft's nature to be worried for long and her mind was soon brimming with wonderful ideas. She would make Lavender a batch of mouthwatering Lavender Creams, Periwinkle was sure to appreciate a selection of Periwinkle Puffs and everyone loved Fairy Fudge. In case anyone was thirsty, she would fill hazel-nut shells with her famous Dandelion and Burdock Juice, created in honor of her two dearest friends. The juice was quite tricky to make—once, Candytuft had stirred in the wrong direction while whispering a charm and the sparkling drink had turned to sludge—so she intended to follow the recipe to the letter.

She stood on tiptoes to reach her petal apron, which was slung over a nearby stem, and glanced around for her beloved recipe book. Not being the tidiest fairy in the Flower Fairies' Garden, Candytuft wasn't worried when she didn't spot it immediately. She looked in all the usual places—beside the cooking pot, in between her spoons and inside her storage shells—but the recipe book was nowhere to be seen. So she looked in all the unusual places too. But there was still no sign of the tattered old recipe book, whose white petal pages curled at the edges and whose words were smudged where she'd accidentally dropped mixture on to them.

And suddenly, Candytuft remembered. She *had* left her recipe book in one of the usual places. It had lain beside her cooking pot, looking—if a fairy were to glance very quickly and not pay too much attention—just like a small heap of white petal handkerchiefs.

"Oh, no," groaned Candytuft. Her shoulders, her wings and even her blonde curls sagged disconsolately.

Her precious book of magical recipes was in the wash.

There wasn't a moment to lose. "Stop!" cried Candytuft, as she sped through the garden, leaving a trail of surprised Flower Fairies in her wake. "Stop! Fire! No, not fire, sorry . . . But stop! *Please*!"

"What on earth is the matter?" asked a very worried Lavender, when Candytuft skidded to a halt beside the stream, almost overbalancing into the water.

"*Please* tell me that you haven't washed my handkerchiefs yet," pleaded Candytuft, her sweet little face flushed bright pink after her cross-garden dash.

Wordlessly, Lavender lifted sodden, white petals from the stream.

Chapter Two
Try and Try Again

Candytuft stared at the spotlessly clean recipe book. The blank white petals seemed to mock her with their emptiness. She sighed forlornly. All of her valuable recipes had vanished—not a single word or a letter remained.

Lavender had been absolutely mortified when she'd discovered what had happened, but Candytuft smiled bravely and tried to look as if it wasn't too much of a problem. "It was my silly fault," she said, with a forced laugh. "It's about time that I invented some new treats anyway!"

But in the privacy of her own plant, her greatest fear bubbled to the surface. "What if I can never make delicious candy again?" she said to herself as a single shiny tear ran down her cheek.

The wasp flew past, pausing to buzz in Candytuft's ear and, for the first time since she'd discovered her mistake, the little Flower Fairy smiled. "You're absolutely right, of course," she told the friendly insect. "I can't let one itsy-bitsy problem like a total lack of recipes spoil things." She squared her shoulders determinedly. "I'll experiment!"

The very first step was to hunt for ingredients. Candytuft put a large sack woven from dried stems over one shoulder and marched purposefully around the Flower Fairies' Garden. And, once she explained her situation to the fairies she met, they fell over themselves to provide her with as many goodies as she could carry.

Crab-apple gave her two fine fruits that she'd stored during the long winter. "They're a little bit sour," she warned. "I like them that way, but you might want to add a smidgen of honey to sweeten them up a little."

"That's a great idea," Candytuft said, carefully tucking the crab apples inside her sack. "Thank you so much."

The round, cuddly fairy who lived in the mulberry bush was reaching into a handful of plump berries when Candytuft passed by. "Oh, there you are!" he called, the perky stem on his dark red cap waving to and fro. "I heard that you needed some tasty morsels and I've collected you a *huge* pile of berries!" He wiped a dribble of berry juice from his chin and cleared his throat guiltily. "That is . . . it *was* a huge pile."

Candytuft stifled a giggle. She knew how much the little fairy loved to eat, and also that he regularly shared his purple-red fruit with the hungry silkworms that lived on his branches. "If you can spare them," she said, "I'd love to take a couple of clusters."

"Is that all?" said Mulberry, relief lighting up his face. "Here you go!" And he tossed two bunches of closely packed fruit down to her.

Candytuft couldn't believe how kind everyone was. She collected bundles of sweet stamens, slivers of silvery bark and heaps of petals. The generous bees gave her a whole, sticky honeycomb too. Her sack was soon bulging. It was extremely heavy too—so heavy that she had to sprinkle a pinch of precious fairy dust on to it to make it lighter for the journey home.

Back at her flower, Candytuft donned her pink-and-white striped petal apron and set to work. Her cooking pot was a sturdy old horse-chestnut case that she'd toughened with fairy magic. It was perfect for cooking because, when it was upended, the spikes poked into the ground so that it didn't wobble. She rubbed the inside with a lime leaf to make sure it was perfectly clean and to add a lovely tangy flavor to the candy.

"And now for my first ingredient!" announced Candytuft, bowing to her small but appreciative audience—Dandelion and Burdock. She broke off seven tiny mulberries and dropped them into the pot.

"Now for my *second* ingredient!" she said, and added a splash of morning dew. "And my third . . ." Essence of plum—a whole handful—tumbled into the pot. She went to dip an acorn cup into the mixture and then swiftly changed her mind.

"What are you doing, Candytuft?" asked Dandelion curiously. He swung on a nearby branch, his dazzling yellow and green outfit and beautiful wings glowing as brightly as the sun.

She paused, her foot in mid-air. "Why, I'm getting in, of course." She grinned broadly at Dandelion's horrified expression and hopped into the cooking pot. "I won't extract the full, delicious flavor of the mulberries simply by stirring," she explained. She stepped lightly from side to side, feeling the tiny berries squish and pop beneath her toes.

"Oh my," said Burdock, his eyebrows arching so high that they looked in danger of floating up, up and away from his forehead. "You did wash your feet, didn't you . . . ?"

Precisely 101 steps later—which was when Candytuft felt that the mixture was just right—she prepared some magic words, wishing desperately that she could have remembered the old ones in her recipe book. She scattered a pinch of fairy dust on to the purple-red surface of the mixture and whispered the new charm . . . "*Softer than cloud, luscious and light, sweets to lift spirits to a dizzying height.*"

Instantly, the mulberry potion thickened, gaining a glossy shine. Candytuft smiled. This was going much better than she'd hoped. Happily, she plunged her hands into the horse-chestnut case and began to roll the mixture into a variety of shapes, laying these gently on to a green leaf to dry. "I shall call these . . . Mulberry Nuggets!" she announced.

"Bravo!" shouted Dandelion and Burdock. "Can we try them?"

Beaming with pride, Candytuft offered them the leafy tray of sticky candy and drifted off into a wonderful daydream where Flower Fairies were crowding round to congratulate her on her new recipe. She hadn't lost her touch, after all. She could still make the best treats in all Flower Fairyopolis!

"Ew!" said Dandelion, looking rather horrified.

Burdock turned a pale shade of green that was remarkably similar to his leggings. "I don't think they're your greatest creation..." he said politely, and hiccupped.

But worse was to come. Candytuft watched in horror as, without a single flap of their wings, Dandelion and Burdock rose above the ground before sailing right up into the air. Too surprised to cry out, their mouths formed Os of astonishment.

"Oh my goodness!" cried Candytuft. Her charm had gone terribly wrong. Somehow, instead of lifting the fairies' spirits to dizzying heights, she'd lifted the Flower Fairies themselves!

She switched immediately into auto-fairy mode and reached for the emergency pinch of fairy dust that was safely hidden in her waistband. *"Fairy dust, fairy dust, back down to earth!"* she cried, flinging the magic sparkles upwards.

She held her breath anxiously. Would this charm work ... or would her best friends be trapped high in the treetops forever?

Chapter Three
Meddlesome Mischief

Fortunately, the power of the Mulberry Nuggets was no match for Candytuft's counter spell, and Dandelion and Burdock floated gently back down to earth. They were very matter-of-fact about the whole adventure and bravely offered to test more of Candytuft's experimental candy.

"It's really rather exciting," said Dandelion, who was always up for new experiences. His twinkling eyes showed that he wasn't in the slightest bit angry.

"But no mulberries," insisted Burdock with a shudder. "Something sweeter next time, please. And not quite so uplifting."

"Oh, of course!" insisted Candytuft, relieved beyond belief that her tasters hadn't deserted her. "I'm sure it won't happen again, you know."

But it did.

The Hazelnut Nougat made Burdock's brown wings turn bright orange—they smelt of orange too, which was very strange. And when Dandelion tried the Silver-Birch Brittle he began to bark like a dog. As for the Fuschia Fondants . . . well, the two Flower Fairies weren't wild about their fingernails turning bright pink. As soon as they could, they made up an excuse and left, to be replaced by more eager fairy volunteers. By now, news of Candytuft's exploits had travelled far and wide.

But there were sweet successes too.

With tiny alterations to her recipe for Mulberry Nuggets, Candytuft created delightful treats that melted on the tongue without sending Flower Fairies shooting up into the trees. Her Crab-Apple Chunks—apple pieces coated with a sweet honey crust—were declared to be irresistible by everyone who tasted them, and the first batch only made the fairies' ears grow a *tiny* bit pointier . . .

Before long, Candytuft had stopped fretting and started enjoying herself instead. She began to realize that she'd been so used to making the same candy from her trusty recipe book over and over again that she'd forgotten what fun it was to create something totally new.

"I'm never going to get stuck in a rut again," she told Celandine fairy, who'd dropped by to sample the latest offerings. "Classic, traditional candy is all very well, but everyone likes a change, don't they? Although . . ." she added, gazing into her cooking pot wistfully, "I do so wish I could rediscover the recipe for Fairy Fudge—"

"C-c-candytuft," interrupted Celandine. Candytuft dipped a finger into the latest mixture—Daisy Chews—and thoughtfully slurped it clean. "Mmm . . ." she said, distracted by the delicious taste. "Yes?" she asked.

There was no reply and Candytuft looked up to see that Celandine was quietly sobbing into a yellow petal handkerchief. "Whatever's the matter?" she gasped. "Oh, I'm so sorry! Here I am, chattering away about myself and I didn't ask how you are . . . Do tell me what's wrong. I'll listen, I really will."

Celandine pushed her beautiful auburn hair away from her face. She sniffed a little and clenched her dainty hands into fists, screwing the handkerchief into a ball as she did so. For a moment, she looked so agitated that Candytuft wasn't even sure she'd be able to speak. But then the words started tumbling out, like water from an underground spring.

"I shouldn't s-s-say," she stammered. "It's just that it's s-s-so upsetting."

"Oh, poor Celandine!" said Candytuft, flinging a slightly sticky arm around her shoulders. "Tell me everything." She led the trembling Flower Fairy to a mossy cushion.

Obediently, Celandine sat down, folding her glorious greeny-yellow wings and spreading the long yellow petals of her skirt carefully around her, while she calmed down. Then, whispering in a voice so quiet that Candytuft had to lean close to hear, she began to speak.

It was a sorry tale indeed. As part of Fairy Friendship Week, Celandine had decided to make some new slippers for Dandelion—his were looking shabby and worn. Rather than bothering him for materials, and to make it even more of a surprise, she'd used her own tough leaves, snipping and shaping the green slippers until they were just right. Now, all she'd needed was a dandelion seed head to make a fluffy pompom for each slipper. For this, she *had* to visit Dandelion—there was no part of her flower that would do.

"S-s-so I went to find him," said Celandine. "But h-h-he was nowhere to be found."

This was no great surprise to Candytuft. She knew how much Dandelion liked to travel. After all, his flower would grow anywhere, so why would he want to live in one place?

"And when I got home—" here, Celandine gave a great, heaving sob— "the slippers were r-r-ruined, torn to shreds!"

"Do you have any idea what happened?" asked Candytuft gently. She was sure there had to be some rational explanation. This sort of thing just didn't happen in Flower Fairyopolis.

"It was D-d-dandelion. He did it!" Celandine burst into tears once again.

For once in her life, Candytuft was speechless with shock and disbelief. Then her chatty tongue wiggled into action once more. "But how do you know?" she asked. "Why would Dandelion ruin a present that you'd made for him?" Dandelion was one of Candytuft's best friends. He wouldn't do such a thing, would he . . . ?

"W-w-when I got back, I found dandelion petals scattered everywhere," Celandine said, her chocolate-brown eyes filled with sadness. "It's the truth," she said. "I can't imagine why he did it, but he *did*, Candytuft. He did."

"We must ask him what happened," said Candytuft firmly. She was a great believer in hearing both sides of a story.

But Celandine vetoed the suggestion at once. "We *can't!*" she cried, utterly horrified by the suggestion. "It's Fairy Friendship Week. We can't accuse another fairy of unneighborly behavior at the friendliest time of the year!"

Chapter Four

More Strange Happenings

Reluctantly, Candytuft agreed that they should let sleeping fairies lie. After she'd dried her tears, Celandine insisted that she wasn't upset anymore—Candytuft didn't believe a word of it—and that she would simply make another pair of slippers for Dandelion. So, furnished with a bundle of freshly made and exceedingly sticky treats, she made her way home.

Thoroughly bemused, Candytuft went back to her cooking pot, where she tried to make sense of it all. "It's just not Dandelion's style," she muttered to herself, adding a smidgen of corn and some yellow stamens to the mixture. "He's kind and he's thoughtful. He helps other fairies, he doesn't upset them."

Fairy footsteps approached. "Talking to yourself again?" asked Burdock, dragging a handful of brown stems laden with bristly burrs. "You need to get out more!" he chortled.

"Not much chance of that, this week," said Candytuft, grimacing. She took the solid lump of candy from her cooking pot and plonked it on to a clean leaf, before rolling it out with a smooth, thick stem. "Well, what do you know, Burdock?" she asked, certain that her friend would entertain her.

"Come on . . . spill the beans. While I'm stuck here, it's up to you to bring the news to me."

"Hmm . . . I'm not sure I should say." Burdock's usually sunny expression darkened. "But I have to tell someone." He crouched down beside Candytuft, who had stopped rolling as soon as she'd heard his tone. "My news isn't good," he went on. "In fact, it's downright dreadful."

"What's the matter?" she asked, feeling distinctly uneasy.

So Burdock explained. As a favor to the other fairies during Fairy Friendship Week, he had decided to provide a complimentary spring-cleaning service. Armed with his trusty burr brush, he had patrolled the garden in search of messy places in need of a good cleaning. And, while each lucky Flower Fairy was away from his or her flower, he'd taken the opportunity to sweep and prune and tidy to his heart's content.

"But what's dreadful about that?" asked Candytuft.

Burdock sighed. "When I'd finished, I revisited each flower, just to admire their loveliness," he said. "But each and every one was as messy as can be. If anything, they were *worse* than before I'd started! And now I just don't know why I bothered. The fairies don't appreciate my friendly behavior at all." He hung his head and absent-mindedly fiddled with the tassels on his burgundy tunic. "There's more," he said reluctantly.

"I found evidence—the culprits dropped their own petals everywhere."

"But who—?"

Burdock shook his head. "I won't say who it is," he said stubbornly.

Candytuft patted her dear friend's shoulder and frowned. Strange things were afoot in the Flower Fairies' Garden, and no mistake. "We should ask around to find out what's going on," she said.

But Burdock was just as reluctant as Celandine to discuss the matter with the rest of the fairies. "What if I'm wrong?" he demanded, gabbling at great speed. "There could be other explanations. What if I got the flowers mixed up? What if a small but very fierce tornado whipped through the garden when my back was turned?"

"How about you take a break?" said Candytuft in her most calming voice. She hastily pressed a few flower shapes from the rolled-flat mixture and gave them to Burdock. "You've had a nasty shock," she said. "Take these Daisy Chews back home and try to relax a little. Let me deal with this."

Burdock nodded and, looking very relieved, scurried away.

Candytuft pondered the facts for a long, long time, but she came no closer to solving the mysteries that Burdock and Celandine had confided in her. All she knew was that the harmony of Fairy Friendship Week was at stake. And if she didn't do something about it, the peace and friendliness that made the Flower Fairies' Garden such a wonderful place to live would be gone forever.

Chapter Five
Mysterious Visitors

For a fairy who was used to roaming around in search of conversation, Candytuft found it hard to believe that she could hear so much gossip by staying in one place. There was no need to go looking for clues. Once they realized that she was confined to her open-air kitchen, the other fairies visited regularly. And they came laden with more strange tales.

Candytuft discovered that Celandine and Burdock weren't the only fairies to suffer bad luck. The petals from one of Rose's most magnificent blooms had been scattered around her rose garden—and she'd found one of Zinnia's unmistakable pink petals amid the disorder. Then someone stole all the fluffy seeds from Dandelion's clocks, so he couldn't tell the time. Dandelion told Candytuft that he'd found one of Celandine's long yellow petals wrapped around a stem and tied in a big, floppy bow.

More and more fairies came to see Candytuft with their tales of woe—all of them highly confidential. Everyone was talking to her about the strange goings on, but no one was talking to each other. Before long, Candytuft knew so many secrets that she barely opened her mouth for fear of blurting any of them out. Instead, she took careful notes. The evidence was sure to come in very handy.

"If only I had enough candy to go round," she muttered to her cooking pot when there was no one within earshot—she could only imagine that there was a lull in the mischief. "Then I could stop making candy and start making enquiries instead." She turned round to check her stockpile of candy and got

the biggest shock of her life. The great heap of
fairy treats stretched so high into the air that
it reached past the top of her flower. "My
goodness," she said. "I *have* been busy . . . "

She had more than enough candy to treat
the whole Flower Fairies' Garden twice—
maybe three times—over!

Candytuft beamed with delight and then
peered into her cooking pot, which contained
a kaleidoscope of pale pink, vivid purple
and snowy white. She was preparing
Candytuft Fudge—a brand-new
concoction of utter deliciousness made
from her very own petals and a few very
secret ingredients that she'd collected on
her expedition around the garden.

"Ahem," said a gruff voice.

Candytuft spun round to face some of the most awkward-looking fairies she'd
ever laid eyes on. There were three of them—a small fairy flanked by two much

heftier companions. All wore curious outfits
made up of emerald, ivy and lime green
leaves, sewn together in a higgledy-
piggledy fashion. And tied on each
of their heads was a large petal bonnet
made from a mishmash of dandelion,
rose, celandine and zinnia petals, with a
burdock burr perched on top. The bonnets
hung low over their brows and entirely
covered their ears, but not their glittery
dark eyes or their pointed noses.

The smallest fairy cleared his throat again. "It's Fairy Friendship Week," he said. "We want to eat your candy. Give us some." One of the bigger fairies nudged him. "Please," he muttered.

Candytuft had never known a fairy to act in this way and she was quite taken aback. But she tried not to let it show and gave a tinkling laugh instead. "But of course," she said, stirring briskly. "Although . . . we fairies usually give presents because we *want* to, rather than being asked for them."

"Candy," growled the little fairy. "Now."

"I haven't seen you around these parts," said Candytuft, biding her time. She wanted to be quite sure of her facts before she pounced. "Have you come far?"

"Yes—" said one of the bigger fairies, but a stern look from the fairy-in-charge silenced him. "Er . . . no."

"We live here," insisted the leader. "We are the fairies. Now, where is that candy? We like treats."

By now, Candytuft's senses were on red alert. She decided to go for it. "You like causing mischief too, don't you?" She stopped stirring, placed her hands firmly on her hips and conjured up her angriest glare, which she directed right at the visitors.

They spluttered with indignation, huffing and puffing like old-fashioned steam trains. "We never . . . how dare . . . mischief?" The smallest fairy was quite beside himself.

"Then how do you explain these?" asked Candytuft, pointing to the collection of petals decorating his bonnet. "Which fairy *are* you, exactly? Where are *your* petals? You seem to be wearing a whole bunch of petals that I know for a fact belong to other Flower Fairies."

At once, all their bravado leaked away. The three suspects hung their heads guiltily. They knew they'd been found out.

"And I suppose you could tell me a thing or two about the mischief that's been going on," said Candytuft. She leant forward and plucked the smallest fairy's bonnet from his head. "Couldn't you, Mr Elf?"

The game was up. On his head was a pair of exceedingly pointy and very long elf ears. These were no Flower Fairies—these were elves!

Chapter Six
Sweet Victory

"Mischief is what we like doing best," explained the smallest elf.

It was much later and the three elves were slurping elderflower tea from hazelnut shells. Much to Candytuft's surprise, she'd found it was very easy to forgive the naughty elves, who kept making her laugh with their odd comments. But all the same, she was determined that they should put things right.

"You've made a lot of fairies very sad indeed," she said seriously. "Your naughtiness has threatened some of the strongest friendships in Flower Fairyopolis. Playing tricks is bad enough, but leaving fake clues so the Flower Fairies would blame each other is shocking behavior. You'll have to make amends." She dealt the final blow. "You'll have to apologize."

"Oh no," said the smallest elf quite insistently. "We're really not very good at saying sorry. We're much better at causing mayhem. We're the elves, you know."

"That's a shame," said Candytuft, daintily sipping her tea. "And I was going to give you some candy to take home with you too. Ah, well . . . never mind."

"Er . . . candy, you say?" the elf laughed nervously. "Well, I suppose we could come to some arrangement—in the interests of fairy friendship, you understand.

Not because we've gone soft."

"Of course not," said Candytuft, quickly turning to her cooking pot to hide her smiles. "Just let me put the finishing touches to my Candytuft Fudge . . ."

The most brilliant idea had popped into her head—an idea so cunning that the elves themselves would have been proud of it. She would lace the candy mixture with an honesty enchantment. When the elves ate the fudge they would feel compelled to be totally truthful.

"Fairy dust, fairy dust, please tell the truth," she whispered, as she sprinkled a generous pinch of fairy dust into the sweet concoction, quickly stirring it in to hide the telltale sparkles. "And that's the whole truth, and nothing but the truth," she added, to be on the safe side.

In less time than it takes a Flower Fairy to flutter their wings, the Candytuft Fudge was ready. And it looked wonderful. Its pink, purple and white marbling swirled through the fudge like a wobbly rainbow. It was shiny and sticky. It was irresistible. It was *perfect*.

"Well, we'd best be off then," said the elves, tripping over their pointy shoes in their eagerness to get their hands on the fudge.

"Please try some before you go," said Candytuft sweetly. "And be sure to visit these fairies first." She gave them a pink petal inscribed with fairy names: Celandine, Burdock, Dandelion, Rose and Zinnia.

The elves nodded. "Mmm . . . mm-mm . . . *mmm* . . . mmm," they said, their mouths far too full of sticky fudge for them to speak

properly. They heaved sacks of sweets on to their shoulders and waved goodbye.

"And don't forget to clean your teeth this evening!" called Candytuft. She hung back for a few seconds before following them at a safe distance. Although she had great faith in her enchanted fudge, she wanted to be absolutely sure that the elves righted their wrongs. Fairy friendship was far too important to leave to chance.

Giggling merrily to themselves, the elves scampered through the garden, so happy that they leapt into the air and tapped their heels together in delight. They reached Celandine's flower first, nestled by the side of a sunny footpath.

"Yoohoo!" called one of the elves, "We've come to tell you the truth!"

He froze, horrified by his own words. "What I mean to say," he corrected himself, "is that we've come to ap—" The little elf clamped his lips shut before he could say the dreaded word. But it slipped out anyway. "Apologize!"

"What's that?" said Celandine. She appeared from behind her flower. In her hands were a pair of half-finished green slippers and a needle and thread.

"He said that we've come to apologize," repeated one of the bigger elves. He shrugged helplessly as the last elf threw him a cross look. "Can't help it, boss," he said. "I know you don't want to tell this lovely fairy that we ruined Dandelion's slippers, but—"

"Shush!" hissed the other elf. "You'll be telling her that we planted fake evidence next!"

"Ooops," said the third elf. "Sorry, Celandine," he said gruffly to the astonished Flower Fairy. "Want some fudge?"

Candytuft hugged herself gleefully. Even from this distance—she was safely hidden behind the lavender bush—she could see that Celandine was thrilled by the revelations.

A gentle smile brightened her glum face. "So it wasn't Dandelion?" Celandine said, as the truth slowly sank in. "It was you all along." She tried to look stern, but was much too nice a fairy to be angry for long. "Well, I think that's very brave of you to tell the truth." She grasped the smallest elf's hand firmly and

pumped it up and down. Then she looked at the candy they'd brought. "And you're delivering Candytuft's gifts too. Well, isn't that the kindest thing."

The elves had the decency to look embarrassed, but seemed to enjoy being on the receiving end of compliments for a change and smiled broadly. "Well, we must dash," said the little elf. "No rest for the wicked." He checked the list and sauntered off in the direction of Burdock's home, his companions following on behind.

Candytuft smiled contentedly as she listened to the astonished cries and cheery laughter that was soon echoing all around as the elves unwittingly revealed all to everyone they met. To think that the Flower Fairies' Garden might by now be riddled with suspicion and lies if she hadn't mixed up her washing! And with that thought Candytuft skipped into the garden to join her fairy friends.

The Song of
the Buttercup Fairy

'Tis I whom children love the best;
  My wealth is all for them;
For them is set each glossy cup
  Upon each sturdy stem.
O little playmates whom I love!
  The sky is summer-blue,
And meadows full of buttercups
  Are spread abroad for you.

Buttercup and the Fairy Gold

by Pippa le Quesne

Chapter One

A Surprise Shower

"This way! Quick!"

Buttercup gasped as a huge drop of rain hit her squarely on the head and then trickled down either side of her face.

She turned and set off for the top end of the meadow, where she knew there was an enormous dock plant growing. It was hard going, running uphill with the rain in her eyes, and Cowslip, who had longer legs, soon caught up. The two Flower Fairies took the last few strides side by side, mindful of the water trickling off the tips of the dock leaves and collecting in murky pools on the ground.

"We're drenched!" exclaimed Cowslip as she lifted a strap over her head and carefully lowered two acorn-shell pots to the ground. Then she burst out laughing as she glanced at her friend.

Buttercup's flaxen hair was plastered to her head, her green stockings and shoes were speckled with mud, and her wings hung limply behind her. She grinned back at Cowslip but was preoccupied with examining the horse-chestnut shell that she had been carrying. When the first drop of rain had plopped on to her nose, Buttercup had plucked some petals and hastily covered her basket. Now she cautiously peeled one back and let out a sigh of relief as she caught sight of the gleaming pile of soft pollen.

Phew! It was safe—and the morning's work hadn't been wasted.

"It's only a shower, and once the sun's out, we'll soon dry off," she said cheerfully, leaning back against the sturdy stalk of the dock.

The huge plant towered way above them, and the two friends were silent for a few minutes, catching their breath and listening to the rain drumming on the broad leaves overhead. Even though it was early summer, it had been hot for the past month or so, and the Flower Fairies knew that *everyone* would be glad of this shower.

"Lucky that we'd nearly finished," remarked Cowslip. She jumped to her feet and then, opening her tawny wings, began to beat them rapidly to get rid of any remaining water. Next she combed through her dark wavy hair with her fingers and shook out her layered yellow skirt.

"You're right," Buttercup agreed, absentmindedly spreading her own wings to let them drip dry. "Harvesting wet pollen is a nightmare. It's impossible to stop it from sticking together in clumps." She hugged her knees happily.

They'd been up since dawn, and she'd already managed to visit nearly every one of the buttercups in the meadow where they lived. And that meant she must have collected enough of her flowers' pollen to keep her stocked up for practically the whole year! All that was left to do was grind it up to make her own special fairy dust and find somewhere secret to store it.

"Wow, I'm starving after all that work," said Cowslip, who had just finished wiping off her bare legs and feet with a scrap of the spongy moss that she'd used to seal her acorn pots. She reached into her skirt pocket and produced a piece of pale yellow honeycomb. "Here—let's share this. It's from Honeysuckle. The bees always give him some in exchange for his flower nectar."

They'd been so absorbed in their harvesting that Buttercup hadn't noticed how hungry she was. Her tummy suddenly rumbled and reminded her that breakfast had, in fact, been hours ago. "Ooh, thanks. I've never tried it before," she said, gratefully taking the chunk of honeycomb that Cowslip held out to her. As soon as she bit into it, the sugary crystals melted on her tongue and filled her mouth with a sweetness more wonderful than anything she could remember tasting. Buttercup was so lost in the sensation that at first she didn't notice that the sound of pouring rain had been replaced by a soft tinkling that was gradually getting louder.

"Come and listen!" called Cowslip, who, with her acorn pots slung over her shoulder, had ventured out from their dock-leaf shelter.

From the top of the sloping meadow you could see the patchwork of farmers' fields that bordered the nearby woodland and the long, straight lane that cut across them.

Buttercup shielded her eyes from the already bright sunshine and peered in the direction that Cowslip was pointing.

132

She couldn't see anything apart from a few birds fluttering in and out of the hedgerows, but coming from the lane was the distinct sound of fairy bells ringing. It was a familiar and welcome sound to them both as it heralded the arrival of one of their dearest friends. She always carried a long, slender stem that held snowy white flowers that nodded and tinkled as she walked.

"Lily-of-the-Valley!" Buttercup shouted happily. "Let's go and surprise her." And without waiting for a response, she bounded down the hill.

Chapter Two
Lost!

"It's *got* to be here somewhere!"

Buttercup had been around the dock plant in both directions and foraged through a tangle of nearby bindweed even though she knew she hadn't been anywhere near it. Now she was poking around in a murky puddle with a twig.

"Oh goodness, oh goodness—what if I've lost all that pollen?" she muttered to herself as she searched.

It wasn't just the heat of the sun that was making Buttercup feel uncomfortably hot. Nor was it the fact that when Lily had headed off home and Cowslip had gone for a nap, she'd remembered her horse-chestnut basket and run all the way back to the dock plant. No, it was because losing her morning's work meant that she wouldn't be able to make any more fairy dust. And, worse than that, the pollen falling into the wrong hands could have disastrous consequences!

It was hopeless, though, tiring herself out by running around in circles looking for it when, in her heart of hearts, the Flower Fairy knew that it was gone. She remembered putting down the basket and checking the pollen just before Cowslip had given her the honeycomb, then they had heard Lily's bells and, as soon as she had recognized them, Buttercup had run off down the meadow without a backward glance. Yup, she had definitely left it behind, and it looked certain that someone had come across it and taken it away.

But who? And where were they now? And how on earth would she begin to find them without any fairy dust? Fairy dust enabled each of the Flower Fairies to work a little magic—not conjure huge spells, but it was a helping hand in times of need. Yet not only had Buttercup completely run out, but now she was faced with the prospect of none at all until a new crop of flowers blossomed in the meadow.

Her heart started to beat very fast, and the young Flower Fairy felt quite overwhelmed by this thought.

"If only Cowslip were here—she'd make me feel better," Buttercup said out loud, thinking about her practical friend. Cowslip was very down-to-earth and always knew what to do. "I could go and find her . . . but there's no time to lose," she went on. "No, I must try and work out exactly what she would do and sort this out by myself."

Buttercup walked to the brow of the hill and took a couple of deep breaths. She needed to focus her thoughts. She needed a plan. She gazed out across the fields and down at the lane below, and then, suddenly, an idea came to her.

* * *

"Jack! Jack! Are you there?"

Buttercup had come to the shady part of the lane where the tall jack-by-the-hedge plants, with their large green leaves and small white flowers, bordered the hedgerow. The Flower Fairy that tended them was never easy to find since his white shirt and breeches, green jerkin, and pearly wings camouflaged him well. It was this very fact that had

given Buttercup the idea to come and seek him out. As the slender fairy was so hard to spot, passersby rarely knew of his presence, and so he picked up a lot of information as he went about his daily business.

Maybe he'd gone to visit the Flower Fairies Garden at the end of the lane. She'd keep looking for a few more minutes, then perhaps that was where she should go, too, and ask for the other fairies' help. But that would mean admitting just how careless she'd been with something so precious. Buttercup gulped.

At that moment, a flash of auburn caught her eye. *Jack?* And then, sure enough, out of the hedgerow popped just the face she was looking for, with its characteristic playful grin and red hair.

136

"Oh, I'm so pleased to see you, Jack," she gushed. "Um, I've misplaced something, and I wondered if you could help? It's my horse-chestnut basket. You wouldn't happen to have noticed anyone passing by this way and carrying one, would you? Oh—and how are you?" Buttercup blushed, suddenly realizing how rude she was, babbling away without even stopping to see how Jack was.

"I'm fine, thanks. Although, actually"—Jack stepped out of the hedge and leaned in close—"between you and me, something rather worrying happened not ten minutes ago."

Buttercup's stomach lurched. "Go on," she said, trying not to let her voice tremble.

"Well, as long as you keep it to yourself . . . Oh, and I'm waiting for a dragonfly to take me to the marshes, so as soon as one turns up I'll have to be off—"

"I absolutely promise." Buttercup beamed her most reassuring smile.

Jack nodded and hopped up on to his plant, where he patted the leaf next to him. "Best stay out of sight," he said. Then, after waiting for Buttercup to join him, he went on.

"What it is, you see—a couple of elves came by about a quarter of an hour ago. They were in an absolute frenzy of excitement and were talking loudly

about some 'fairy gold' that they'd found. Now as you and I well know, there's no such thing as fairy gold—that's just a human fable. But they were ever so pleased with their find and were deciding what to do with it. They seemed pretty sure that they could use it to 'buy' themselves some fairy secrets. That's when I really pricked up my ears. Then one of them said that he'd heard there was a Flower Fairy fair tonight, it being a full moon and all. He suggested that they disguise themselves as a couple of us, go along to the fair, and see how they could get the 'gold' to work in their favor. He felt sure they'd find out all sorts and maybe even leave with some special fairy magic.

"Now, I have no idea what exactly it is that they found—because I stayed well out of sight—and it may well be totally harmless, but I reckon it's better to be safe than sorry. That's why I'm off to warn Kingcup and Queen of the Meadow that Flower Fairyopolis may be in real peril. If that dragonfly doesn't turn up in a minute then I'll just have to set off for the marshes on foot."

At that moment, Buttercup, who was deep in thought and had listened to every word with absolute horror, snapped herself out of her trance.

"No . . . no, Jack, it's fine." She spoke slowly so as not to convey the panic that was rising up inside her. "I know what they were talking about, and it really is no problem. It's all a silly misunderstanding and nothing to worry anyone else about. You know what the elves are like—they probably *knew* that you were listening and were trying to trick you."

She took a deep breath. "So I'll catch up with them—and if I'm wrong I'll be certain to get some help. And"—she paused, making her mind up on the spot— "I'm going to the fair tonight, anyway, so I can make doubly sure that they don't get up to any mischief. Okay?"

Then, without really giving Jack a moment to reply, she jumped down from her perch. He looked pretty perplexed by her forceful speech, but Buttercup decided that acting confidently might do the trick to convince him. So, after waving good-bye, she began to stride off purposefully down the lane. And, when she dared to look back, she saw that although Jack was shaking his head in confusion, he was sending away the dragonfly that had just turned up.

Chapter Three
Fairy Gold

As Buttercup fluttered away, she tried to make sense of the tangle of thoughts in her head. Her heart had skipped a beat when Jack-by-the-Hedge uttered the words "fairy gold." You see, although pretty much everyone in Flower Fairyopolis would tell you that there was no such thing, she knew differently.

Every summer when Buttercup's flowers blossomed, she would painstakingly polish the bright yellow petals until the whole meadow shone with a carpet of dazzling gold. Then, obeying the most important Flower Fairy rule and keeping herself hidden, she would wait for her special visitors—humans.

Buttercup's wings ached, and the glowworm lantern that she'd hooked over her arm felt very heavy. Added to that, it was tiring concentrating on where she was going and trying to work on a plan at the same time. Oh, how she wished she was whiling away an afternoon watching the children playing.

Not far to the woodland now, she told herself, checking her progress. *You can do it!*

On more than one occasion she'd seen a child pick one of her bowl-shaped flowers and hold it up under another's chin. Apparently, if the gold reflected on their skin it meant that they liked butter. This always made Buttercup giggle, since she didn't even know what butter was!

"Gold knots, meadow cup, cuckoo flower . . . Gold knots, meadow cup, cuckoo flower," she recited, finding that it helped her focus her mind as she flew.

These were the different names that humans called her flowers. But mostly, because they longed to meet the magical creatures that lived among them, they made up stories about the fairies, and their favorite name for buttercups was 'fairy gold'.

At that moment, Buttercup touched down on the ground and, just as she did, a thought popped into her head. "If I know those crafty elves, they've been spying," she said out loud. "And I bet when they came across my basket of pollen, they thought they'd hit the jackpot."

She was standing on the edge of the woodland now, looking around for the clump of red-and-white toadstools that marked the path she needed to take. The thought of the elves having in their possession something so dear to her was just too awful.

"But then," she said, as it slowly dawned on her, "they don't know that it makes fairy dust, and that's more precious than anything they could possibly imagine!"

This was a closely guarded secret that only the Flower Fairies knew, and one that the elves were yet to discover. All of a sudden, she felt much better, and having located the spotted toadstools, Buttercup set off through the trees.

The monthly fair took place in a secret glade, and although she'd never been before, she knew how to find it. It was said to be a wonderful occasion, similar to the daily market where the Flower Fairies traded and sold their wares, but special because it took place after dark and only on the night of the full moon. Also, there was lively music and dancing to look forward to. But best of all, both Kingcup and Queen of the Meadow were rumored to always make an appearance.

Lily-of-the-Valley had recently gone along for the first time, and she'd come back bubbling over with enthusiasm. She'd promised Buttercup that as soon as she was old enough to stay up all night, the two of them would go together *every* month. Now Buttercup was not only going to the fair but she was finding her way there all by herself! As the little Flower Fairy jogged along the path, she couldn't help but feel a tingle of excitement.

Buttercup shivered and pulled the oak-leaf wrap more tightly about her. *There's nothing to be scared of,* she told herself.

The rain shower had given way to another scorching day, but once the sun sunk below the horizon, it had turned into a cool, cloudless evening. She'd put on the cloak to hide her striking butterfly wings and distinctive gold dress from the sharp-eyed elves, and now she was glad of the extra layer.

Buttercup stood at the mouth of the tunnel that ran through the center of a thicket and indicated the final leg of her journey. Her lantern only produced a very soft light, and as she peered into the passageway, all she could see was inky blackness.

"On the other side of this is the fair, where there'll be lots of friendly faces." Buttercup took a deep breath. "Besides, you've got a very important job to do." And without further ado, she plunged bravely into the darkness.

At first, she couldn't even see the end of her nose, and so she held out her arms to make sure she didn't bump into anything. Yet the thought of something else being in the tunnel made her even more jumpy. So to calm her nerves, Buttercup concentrated on counting each step as she went, telling herself that she'd reach the other side in no time. And sure enough, she hadn't even reached thirty when a dim glow became visible up ahead. With relief, she quickened her pace, and seconds later she emerged from the thicket to find herself standing in a clearing.

Chapter Four
A Magical Place

Buttercup gasped. Nothing could have prepared her for the magnificent sight that met her eyes.

The circular glade was bathed in shimmering light from the perfect disc of pearly moon that hung in the night sky. All around the perimeter were multicolored stalls adorned with garlands of fragrant flowers and displaying goods of every description. Everywhere Buttercup looked there were Flower Fairies chattering happily away—some that she knew and was glad to see and others that she'd never seen before, but all of them friendly and welcoming.

The most exquisite scent hung in the air—the delicate perfume of the flowers mingled with spices and herbs and things fresh from the oven. Above the hum of cheery voices came the sound of chiming bells. And there, in the very center of the glade, were Harebell and Lily-of-the-Valley, weaving gracefully in and out of an arch made entirely of entwined clematis, shaking their bells as they danced.

Mesmerized, Buttercup slowly began to move from stall to stall. The first table she stopped at was piled high with lusciously ripe summer fruits, while the next was laden with mouthwatering cakes and seeds; a third sold intricately carved wooden instruments, and at the fourth were the prettiest shoes that Buttercup had ever seen, all lined up in neat rows. Next, she found herself drawn to a treasure chest of trinkets, baubles, and ornaments, and before she could help herself, she was absorbed in picking out a pretty necklace that would match her dress.

"It's Buttercup, isn't it? What are you doing here?"

"Hmm?" replied Buttercup, still engrossed.

"Wakey, wakey!"

With a start, Buttercup came to her senses and looked up.

Standing in front of her was a slight fairy dressed in a pretty white tutu skirt and a grayish-green bodice. She looked quite wild with her chestnut hair hanging in her eyes and her bare feet, but Buttercup knew that she lived in the Flower Fairies Garden, where her ordered flowers lived in the borders closest to the human house. It was Pink.

"Hello! Sorry—I didn't mean to ignore you. I was making an important decision." Buttercup laughed, nodding toward the collection of accessories that she had been sorting through.

"I understand," replied Pink good-naturedly. "It's wonderful here, isn't it? My brother and I always come with Tansy. We make the finishing touches to her dresses with our pinking shears." She pulled out a pair of the special scissors that cut zigzag edges into hems or cuffs and gave her flowers their unique crinkly appearance. "But I haven't seen you here before. Have you got a stall this time?"

"No, I just . . . Oh dear, I'd forgotten why I'm here . . . " Buttercup had become so entranced by her new surroundings that she'd completely lost sight of her mission. "Listen, Pink—I've got to go. I'll explain later!" she called over her shoulder as she began to push her way through the throng.

There appeared to be double the amount of fairies that there had been when Buttercup arrived, and since she wasn't very tall, she couldn't see over their heads to the other side of the clearing. *What if I'm too late?* she said to herself, frantically searching for something to stand on. It would take far too long to visit each individual stall, and since everyone was moving around, she'd never be able to make sure she'd checked the whole glade for the elves.

Short of standing on a table and drawing attention to herself, Buttercup couldn't see anything immediate that would give her the height that she needed. Her heart began to race, and the palms of her hands felt clammy as she hunted for a solution. As she loosened the collar on her cloak and then lifted her arms to get some air underneath it, she realized how ridiculous she was being.

I've got wings, of course! She took a couple of steps back to the edge of the clearing where the shadow of the trees would obscure her. Then, throwing the cloak to the ground, she beat her wings, and seconds later was hovering just above the crowd.

Now although elves are similar creatures to Flower Fairies—in that they, too, are no more than four inches high—if you look closely, there are some obvious differences. Their wings and ears are extra pointy, they have muddy bare feet and unkempt straggly hair, and they are never without their pointed green hats. Jack had said that the naughty elves he'd overheard were plotting to disguise themselves, but Buttercup felt sure that they wouldn't be clever enough to cover up all of their telltale features.

147

She'd been scanning the crowd for a good five minutes now, but to no avail. She kept spotting someone, thinking she'd found an elf, and then get a proper look and recognize them as a Flower Fairy.

"Aha! Look at *those* pointed ears—that must be one of them. Nope, patterned wings—it's Herb Robert. What about . . . No, I know that face well—it's Periwinkle."

And then there was Snapdragon and Cornflower, Crocus and Honeysuckle . . . It was hopeless. Buttercup felt defeated.

With a heavy heart, she admitted to herself that she'd made a mistake. "I should never have tried to sort this out on my own," she said, her eyes filling with tears. "There's nothing else for it. I shall just have to tell the others how foolish I've been."

Buttercup had just begun to look around for her friend Lily when she was distracted by a tantalizing smell drifting up from the stall below her. She glanced down. There—in an eye-catching scarlet dress—was Poppy, setting out bowls of toasted seeds coated in sticky nectar. It was her infamous popcorn that no one could resist!

And neither could this hungry, tired Flower Fairy. She landed lightly on the ground and hurried to join the line that was already forming. Her mouth watering, Buttercup waited patiently for her turn, ready to hand over the single fairy coin that she had in her skirt pocket.

Just then, her attention was caught by the two fairies who were talking loudly at the front of the line. She didn't recognize them, but their clothes seemed very familiar . . .

They both wore green leaf shirts with flamboyant collars and irregular hems paired with russet breeches and . . . *Sycamore?* Poppy had just finished piling two bowls high with popcorn, and one of the fairies was reaching into a basket that hung on the far side of him.

Hang on a minute. Something about them bothered Buttercup, and she desperately tried to work out what it was. She didn't know the Tree Fairy very well, but she was certain that he didn't have a brother. And—that was it—Sycamore definitely didn't wear a hat! It had to be the elves!

"Excuse me, excuse me. Sorry for pushing, but it's very important. You have to trust me—" Buttercup's heart was racing as she began nudging her way to the front as politely as she could without making a scene.

"Well," Poppy was saying, examining the pile of soft, gleaming powder that the elf held out in his cupped hands. "This is a very irregular way to be paid and it still leaves me with all the grinding to do, but it's always good to have an extra supply of fairy—"

"Wait!" shouted Buttercup. Without knowing it, Poppy was about to give away the one secret most prized by the whole of Flower Fairyopolis!

Chapter Five
Out of the Blue

"What on earth's the matter?" said Poppy, taken aback by the sudden disturbance.

"It's them! They're, they're . . ." Buttercup stammered, lost for words as it suddenly occurred to her that it would take too long to explain what was going on.

The elves seemed to have caught on to the fact that their cover was blown. The elf who'd offered Poppy the pollen was hastily brushing it off his hands into the chestnut-shell basket while the other was already backing away from the stall, looking sheepish. It wouldn't take them a moment to slip away, and not only would it be the last that Buttercup saw of her pollen, but surely once all of the elves put their heads together they'd discover its magical properties before too long. She was going to have to do something—and fast! But what?

All the fairies were talking at once now, and there was such a din that she couldn't think straight. Just then, a long deep note resonated. It cut through the hullabaloo and stopped everyone, including the elves, in their tracks. Buttercup spun around. There, entering the glade, was a grand procession led by a fairy dressed in burgundy and royal blue and blowing a horn. It was Bugle announcing the arrival of Kingcup and Queen of the Meadow!

As the eager Flower Fairies huddled back against the stalls to enable the regal visitors to make their way into the center of the clearing, Buttercup found herself face-to-face with the elf carrying her basket. His eyes widened as he took a good look at her and, realizing who she was, clutched the chestnut shell close to his chest so that the gold pollen reflected on his usually sallow skin. It was at that moment that Buttercup remembered something.

When it came to pollen, elves and humans had one thing in common. Of course, it would involve sacrificing every last speck of her precious harvest, but it would mean that the Flower Fairies' secret remained safe.

It didn't take Buttercup a second to make up her mind. Taking the deepest breath she could manage, she stepped toward the elf and blew with all her might. The force of the puff lifted the pollen clean out of the basket and sent it flying straight into the elf's face. There was a moment in which he looked surprised, and then his nose began to twitch . . . and then he let out an enormous sneeze.

"*Aaa-choo!*" Followed by another even louder one. "*AAA-CHOO!*"

And before he could stop himself, the elf was having a sneezing fit and everyone had turned their attention from the king and queen of Flower Fairyopolis to the impostor in their midst. You see, some humans and *all* elves are allergic to pollen, whereas fairies hardly ever sneeze – and *never* because of pollen!

"Elves!" Poppy exclaimed. "Oh my goodness, Buttercup—that's what you were trying to tell me. But how did you know?"

Buttercup glanced at the assembly of fairies gathered around her and blushed. It was time that she explained what a horrible mess she had got herself into. "Well, Cowslip and I got up very early this morning . . ." she began.

"So, this must be the culprit," a booming voice interrupted.

And there, approaching Poppy's stall, was Kingcup, arm-in-arm with Queen of the Meadow. At this, Buttercup's knees gave way beneath her, and, bursting into tears, she sat down hard on the ground.

Chapter Six
Most Precious of All

Queen of the Meadow had the most gentle expression that Buttercup had ever seen. She wasn't at all as the young Flower Fairy had expected. Her feet were bare, her gown was a plain sleeveless smock, and on her head she wore no crown. Her face was framed with a cloud of blonde hair, and around her neck was a string of simple green pearls. But she had a natural elegance about her and a calming presence that made her seem incredibly wise. She had surprised Buttercup by sinking to the ground herself and putting a comforting arm around her. "Now, now," she said kindly. "Dry your eyes. There's nothing at all for you to be upset about. You stopped the elves from getting away with more of their usual mischief."

When Queen of the Meadow put it like that, it made things sound very straightforward, but Buttercup thought she was just being nice. She glanced up at Kingcup, too shy to meet the handsome king's gaze.

"But, Your Majesty called me a culprit—and I am." Her lip trembled, and she fought back a whole new batch of tears. "I mean," she said, lowering her voice, "I may have stopped the elves from actually getting away with my pollen, but it was my fault that they had it in the first place. My carelessness nearly caused a catastrophe for the whole of Flower Fairyopolis."

At that, Kingcup roared with laughter. "I wasn't calling *you* a culprit! I was talking about that roguish fellow!" he exclaimed, cocking his head in the direction of the elf, who had collapsed in a heap at the edge of the glade after his violent sneezing fit. "No, you're to be congratulated both on your quick thinking and your selflessness. You've done very well."

For the first time since that morning, Buttercup almost felt like smiling, but she hadn't told them quite everything yet.

"Yes, but it was stupid of me to try and sort it all out on my own. I was too embarrassed to ask for help, and I stopped Jack from coming to warn you." She looked down at her rain-streaked shoes. "I promise I've learned my lesson, though. And now that I've lost all my pollen, I won't have any fairy dust for a good long while. So whenever I'm in need of some, I shall remember that it is entirely my own fault."

There was a chuckle, and when Buttercup looked up, she saw that Queen of the Meadow had joined in with Kingcup's laughter. "Oh, my dear, you are very honest and sweet, but aren't you forgetting how generous Flower Fairies are?" she said. "You just wait and see, but I don't think it'll be long before you're busy making your own fairy dust again!"

Poppy had retrieved Buttercup's cloak and given her a bowl of her delectable popcorn and a cup of chamomile tea. She sat and chatted to her whenever there was a lull at her stall and, despite not knowing exactly what the queen meant, Buttercup began to feel quite cheerful.

The elves had been sent home after a stern telling-off, but Kingcup and Queen of the Meadow—who came from the marshes, too—were used to their antics and assured everyone that really they meant no harm. Besides, after all that terrible sneezing, it seemed unlikely that they'd go near any pollen for a long time! Then, as Bugle started up a tune on his horn, the king took the queen by the hand and led her to the center of the clearing, and soon the glade was filled with whirling, twirling Flower Fairies.

Buttercup was too exhausted by the day's events to join in the festivities, but she happily watched. She was determined not to miss any aspect of the magical fair but, as the dancing gave way to tranquil singing, she felt her eyelids becoming heavier and heavier, and soon she was struggling to stop them from closing.

"Buttercup."

A soft voice broke into the Flower Fairy's dream, and when she opened her eyes it took her a moment to get her bearings.

Lily-of-the-Valley was standing in front of her. *Where was she?*

Then she noticed the hive of activity behind her friend and realized that she was still in the glade and must have drifted off to sleep. Fingers of gray were creeping into the dark sky as dawn approached and everyone was busily packing up the fair.

Lily smiled. "I've got something to show you—come on." And, beckoning for Buttercup to follow, she darted ahead and disappeared into a nearby copse.

The sky was rapidly changing now, moving through a kaleidoscope of pink and orange hues, until eventually it settled on the clean blue of a new day.

"Look—over there," Lily said, pointing toward a pine tree that had just emerged from the gloom. "Go on," she added reassuringly.

Buttercup followed her gaze—and there, at the base of the tree, was a patch of bright yellow flowers. Buttercups! She couldn't believe her eyes! And wait . . . there also appeared to be what looked like a scroll of parchment.

"It's for you," Lily said, smiling broadly. "Now, I've got to go and help the others, but come and find me when you're ready to go back to your meadow." And without giving Buttercup a chance to ask what was going on, the light-footed fairy opened her wings and fluttered off toward the clearing.

Not knowing what to expect, the young Flower Fairy hesitated for a few seconds. Then, with trembling hands, she picked up the parchment, unrolled it, and began to read:

Dear Buttercup

We, the undersigned, promise that all of us will search our own corner of Flower Fairyopolis until we find some more buttercups. When we do, each one of us will bring you a parcel of pollen to help you make your own special fairy dust.

Your friends forever,

Lily, Poppy, Crocus, Honeysuckle, Harebell, Tansy, Pink, Snapdragon

(and so the list went on)

"This is what Queen of the Meadow meant!" Buttercup gasped.

Completely overwhelmed, she sat down on the woodland floor and reflected for a moment on all that had happened to her since Cowslip had woken her the previous morning.

As she watched the first rays of sunshine light up the clump of golden buttercups, she felt glad that she would have some of her beloved pollen after all. Yet, glancing down at the parchment that was still in her hands, Buttercup realized that she had just learned the real meaning of fairy gold. The most precious thing a Flower Fairy could ever have was friends—and no matter how hard they tried, that was something the elves would never be able to steal!